NOT MINE TO LOVE

FAMILY MATCHMAKER

BOOK THREE

SUMMER COOPER

LOVY BOOKS

Lovy Books Ltd
20-22 Wenlock Road
London N1 7GU

Cover by SC Creative

I couldn't help myself. I was feeling naughty. I settled into his lap and grazed my hips against his crotch. He groaned and clamped his hands around the small of my back.

"If you keep this up, I won't be able to control myself."

"That's the whole point, Julius. I don't want you to control yourself." I took off my shirt then and let it fall to the floor. I wasn't wearing a bra.

He seemed pleased as he greedily brought my body forward, bringing one nipple into his mouth roughly. His mouth felt so good. He moved on to the next nipple, bringing pain and pleasure again together in one place.

I loved the feel of his mouth against my skin. I loved the way my body responded to him. My body was his.

I stared into his eyes as he slowly lowered me onto his member. I spread my legs further to accommodate his thickness until he was fully enveloped inside me. I sighed as I began to ride him, enjoying the feel of him pressing into me, stretching me, molding my sex to his. He felt even bigger today, and I didn't know how much pleasure I could take.

I came quickly and hard, gasping his name as I fell forward on his chest.

"I love you..." he said against my ear.

I tensed. Those were the words I wanted to hear, but why didn't my heart respond with joy upon hearing them. Instead, all I felt was fear.

"You can't love me," I found myself saying back.

"What?"

"You can't love me."

"But I do."

I moved to get off him, to break our physical connection because I couldn't take the emotional connection that was clearly between us. I loved him, but I wasn't allowed to love him.

I jumped up quickly and he sat up instantly, grabbing my hand.

"Wait—"

"I can't love you, Julius."

"Can't or won't?"

"Doesn't matter." I pulled my clothes on, and he did

the same. He walked to the door, waiting for me to stop him, waiting for me to return the love he so readily gave.

Instead, I let him walk out the door. I closed the door behind him and blinded by tears I didn't even know were there, I sat on the couch and cried.

1

————————

$\mathcal{I}$ leaned forward, looked left and then right and then left again. Now was my chance, I thought to myself as I walked down the hall with my shoes in my hand as quickly as I could. After all, I couldn't pick up speed in heels no matter how hard I tried.

"What's up, sexy?" said an obviously inebriated dude as I quickly walked by him. I couldn't help myself; I flashed him a smile over my shoulder, but kept on moving. After all, I couldn't be caught at a college dorm. That would be way too embarrassing and maybe illegal? I wasn't sure. I hadn't gone to law school like I expected, so my knowledge of law was lacking.

I made my way out of the dorm without hearing too many additional comments about my body which I sort of appreciated since I was a lot older than the kids I just came across. I couldn't believe it. I was twenty-five-years-old and still hadn't gotten my act together.

And for some reason, I thought being past the prime of twenty made me more respectable. Funny. I wasn't exactly doing anything respectable at the moment. I was being paid a flat fee to take pictures of a probable cheating spouse by a P.I. that I worked for every now and then. The work made me feel a little dirty, but I needed it. Being a full-time photographer didn't mean I earned much. I shared a crappy apartment with my dad. I didn't have a real career. I was a divorcee. I was pretty much a loser by most people's standards. I was happy that I was an introvert who didn't talk to most people because then I didn't have to explain that I was twenty-five and still had no idea what I wanted in life.

When I finally made it back to my car, I sighed and looked in the mirror, hoping to see that I was presentable enough to show up to Meredith's school program in what I was currently wearing. I pulled at my mini-dress and pretended that I didn't notice that every tug made more of my cleavage show. Oh well. My hair looked respectable, at least. I studied my reflection, looking for telltale signs that I hadn't actually slept last night. I had huge blue eyes, and they looked even bigger in the mirror courtesy of the makeup I had applied last night but hadn't bothered to wipe off. I hated makeup, but I had assumed rightly that the college guys would more than likely let me hang out with them if I looked like a co-ed.

I brushed a hand through my hair and teased my curls. I had spent a significant amount of time with my head pressed against a dorm room window, just trying my best to get the right angle to catch the professor making out with his mistress. My hair had still gotten in the way even though last week I had cut my massive blonde curls back so that I would look a little less like a Disney princess and more of a respectable adult. I still got mistaken for a high-schooler, but maybe that was a good thing.

Speaking of school, I looked down at my phone and groaned. I was going to be late. I had to be at Meredith's school in under thirty minutes, but there was no way I would make it there in time if I went home to change first. I sniffed at my underarms and shrugged. I smelled okay. I could still make it if I skipped a shower.

I was totally feeling pretty smug. I had finally gotten the photos I needed. After a week of following the professor around and trying to catch him in the act with not one but two of his students, I was a little discouraged when I kept coming up with nothing, but it all worked out. I now had incriminating photos of him doing some naughty things in a car and on his desk with two women who definitely didn't fit his wife's description.

Getting the pictures had meant befriending a bunch of fraternity members and moving from one dorm room to another, trying to get evidence of the professor in action. That part wasn't fun. Most of the rooms smelled like dirty gym socks, old pizza, and worse things that I didn't want to think about. A few of the students had even run by me naked, but I kept my eyes trained on the window, and it paid off. Around five am, I caught the professor doing all sorts of things and then politely escorting each co-ed to her car. How bold he was, or maybe it was arrogance since he didn't think he would get caught. I then waited a few hours until the professor left his office before making my getaway.

As I drove to Meredith's school, the smugness I felt earlier disappeared and was replaced by embarrassment. I felt terrible that I was going to show up dirty and kind of smelly to her performance. But it was either that or miss it. And I wasn't going to miss it for anything. I told Meredith I would be there, and I intended to keep my promise even if I was dressed kind of slutty and smelling like last night's leftovers with a hint of sweati-ness thrown in.

Meredith was my ex-husband's daughter and kind of my best friend. I didn't relate very well to most people, so I had few friends. Most of the men I met just wanted to get in my pants. And most women didn't even take the time to get to know me. They just assumed because of the way that I looked that I was flighty and conceited and probably not very smart. They assumed I was the type of woman who used my body to get what I wanted. I mean, sometimes I did. I flirted with the frat boys to get access to their frat house which was directly across from the professor's office.

But the truth was, I was too shy and unsure of myself to be conceited. I just sort of stumbled through life trying to figure it all out as I went along. I didn't know what I wanted out of life, but I knew I was tired of being broke and clueless. I thought earning my bachelor's degree would have at least led me to a career, but I floundered around for years after earning my degree taking random temp jobs, trying to figure out where I fit in the world.

It was like I was stuck in a rut and didn't know what to do about it. I had gone to school. I had done what I was supposed to do, and now I was going nowhere fast. I had a degree and no skillset. I was kind of unemployable after college which was why I decided to take a continuing education course, but instead of just taking something practical like an accounting software course, I signed up for photography. If that course had been graded, I would have barely passed. I didn't even retain much from it. I just liked taking pretty pictures. And I found work on Craigslist with the P.I. firm. She promised me a couple hundred bucks per assignment. I needed a couple hundred bucks. I was sick of being unemployed and living with my dad.

Not that I didn't love my dad. I just felt we both needed our own space.

"Dad," I grumbled to myself. I needed to call him to tell him I was alright. He was probably really worried about me. But I was a stickler for not using my phone while driving, so I didn't dare call or text him now while I was on the highway. For at least the hundredth time, I regretted that I hadn't taken my ex, Tom, to court for alimony. Who was I kidding? I was glad I didn't have to deal with Tom or his money on a monthly basis. Dealing with Tom's nonsense had already aged me a million years if not more.

But gosh it would have been sweet to have a car with Bluetooth technology and then I could just tell the car to call my dad and it would. Instead, I was driving around in a car that was at least half my age, that I also happened to share with my dad. So it wasn't even technically my car.

I texted him quickly to tell him I was alright while stopped at a light. I was young and unemployed, but I wasn't stupid. I had the attention span of a gnat, so there was no way I would text and drive.

When I pulled up to Meredith's fancy private school, I hoped out of my car and headed in the direction of the theatre which was housed in the school's Fine Arts

Center. When I was Meredith's age, I attended a rundown public school in the heart of the city. I felt my entire school could have fit in the Fine Arts building of Meredith's school. It was a little snooty and I did get a few looks, well more than a few, as I made my way to the Fine Arts building.

The ushers opened the doors as I approached, and I caught one staring at my clothes. Feeling self-conscious, I tugged at the hem of my dress and tried to ignore her look of disapproval. I was sure I was going to be talked about at the next PTA meeting.

Inside, the lights were dimmed, but the show hadn't begun yet. I scanned the audience as best as I could. I was able to see at least somewhat. I searched for Dana, Meredith's mom, and found her seated toward the front of the audience. I slowly made my way toward her, trying to navigate the best I could in my heels. The narrow steps leading to the front of the audience was making that quite difficult. We had an unusual relation-ship, Dana and I. We didn't hit it off when we first met. After all, I was the woman Dana was convinced her husband left her for. But when it became clear that I was just as much a victim of Tom's charms, she warmed up to me. Dana had the whole "girl next door" look about her. She was cute even if she didn't know it or appre-ciate her looks. And frankly, I think she looked great for a mother of three. She went on and on about how she was already starting to get wrinkles, but that was only in her head.

"Hi," I said, sitting down next to her.

She smiled at me and said, "Glad you could make it." And then she sniffed the air. "Is it just me or does something around here smell like frat boy funk?"

I shifted away from her and sniffed the air as if I didn't know the smell was coming from me. I looked away and said with a shrug, "I don't smell anything."

I was literally a dirty liar, but my response seemed to appease Dana who shot a look toward a guy in front of us wearing a sports jersey and scratching at his hair which left flakes on his shoulder.

"I bet it's him," she whispered to me before turning her attention elsewhere as the lights darkened in the theatre. "Oh, oh, it's about to start," she whispered excitedly. I smiled and looked at the stage as the lights dimmed further in the auditorium.

An angelic voice sounded from the stage, and I smiled as I instantly realized that voice was Meredith's. The spotlight shone down on her then and I watched her sing, envying her self-confidence. She had practiced at least a million times with me. I wasn't much of a singer, but I had been in chorus all four years of high school. I frowned. High school seemed like just yesterday, but it was actually nearly a decade ago. I didn't know why I found that thought depressing, but I did.

No matter. I smiled, hoping that smiling would make me feel better and it did. Thank god for all those self-help books I loved to read. Dana thought they were just junk, but I swore by them.

Meredith finished her number, and I couldn't help myself. I jumped up and clapped. And then I started cheering. Dana moved slightly away from me. I was sure she was trying to distance herself from my overenthusiasm, but what could I say? I was impressed. More than that... I was sooo proud.

Eventually, I sat and tried to clap ardently for the other students who were performing for the talent show. Meredith wasn't actually competing. She was the host. She was so great. She was everything that I had wanted to be when I was her age, but everything that I totally wasn't.

The show came to an end about two hours later. I didn't even know who won since I had stopped paying attention after the first half hour, but that didn't stop me from cheering for the winner.

"I'm going to go meet up with Meredith," Dana said. "You coming?"

I loved that Dana let me continue to be part of Meredith's life, but I understood there were some moments that she wanted to just share with her daughter, and I felt this was one of them.

"You go ahead. I'll wait for you guys here."

I hadn't been very close to my mom growing up, so mother and daughter time was kind of sacred to me. Not that I regretted not spending time with my mom. According to the Internet, she was a narcissist. Which probably explained why I married a narcissist. I had read that on the Internet too.

I sat on the steps outside of the school in the most ladylike way I could manage as I waited for Meredith and Dana to come out. I got a few looks, but I ignored them. All that mattered was that I was there for Meredith. At least that's what I was telling myself. I hated to be embarrassed, and I hated to be disliked. If my life was a book, I think my high school literature teacher would say that I was a character who was tragically flawed.

I didn't feel flawed though. Yeah, I didn't really have any money, or a spouse for that matter, but when I had all those things I hadn't exactly been ecstatic. I had been just the opposite: miserable. But now, I was single and maybe a little lonely and very much broke, but I was definitely not miserable.

"Hey, did you get those pictures?" asked a familiar voice. A voice that was kind of the epitome of misery.

I turned toward the voice, surprised to see my employer standing there. "Leona," I said surprise clear in my voice as I stood to greet her with a smile she didn't return. "What are you doing here?"

"My grandson goes here," she said shortly. "So did

you get the pictures?" She was always straight to the point. She was in her late sixties, had red hair, wore too much makeup and had a little bit of a smoker's voice. She intimidated me. But I think I was intimidated by at least seventy-five percent of the people I met.

"Yeah, I got them."

"Good," she said before coughing and spitting something out into the bushes nearby. Other parents gave her disapproving looks, but no one dared reprimand her. That was smart. Leona wasn't one to be crossed.

"Stop by my office tomorrow. I have another job for you."

I didn't get a chance to reply because she turned around and walked away.

"Friend of yours?" Dana asked, appearing next to me with Meredith by her side.

"Nope."

"Was that your boss? The private investigator?" Meredith asked.

"Yep, how'd you guess?"

She shrugged, "I don't know. She just has a cagey look about her. Plus, I saw her spit in the bushes. I sort of feel like that's something a real private investigator would do."

I laughed and said, "And great job by the way."

She beamed up at me. "Thank you. I had a great coach."

"Thanks for helping her. It was sweet of you," Dana added.

"It was my pleasure."

"Enough about me," Meredith said, placing her hands on her hips. "Tell me about your next assignment. Is it another dirty, cheating, no-good husband?"

She sounded so grown up which made me want to laugh. I shrugged. "Probably. It seems like every case is a no-good, cheating husband."

Dana and I exchanged a look. We were both thinking of the ex we had in common. He swore up and down that he hadn't cheated on us, but if there was anything we knew about Tom, it was that he loved to lie.

"Do you think your next assignment will take a lot of time?"

"Why the question? Do you need me for something?"

She nodded and then shook her head.

I laughed, "So is that a yes or a no?"

"It's a maybe ... you see Danny Schultz's aunt, well great-aunt, she's super old. Anyway, she's super stressed because her daughter is going to marry a rascal."

I laughed. "Rascal? What does that even mean?"

She shrugged. "That's what Danny told me. I think a rascal is a jerk. I don't know."

"So what does that have to do with me?"

"Well…" She looked hesitant and continued as fast as

she could. "Well, I sort of told Danny what you do, and he told his aunt and now she wants to meet you..."

"What?"

Dana frowned. "What did I tell you about volunteering us for anything and everything?"

"It's for a good cause."

Dana couldn't hold back a laugh. "This kid is hilarious."

"I am," she said seriously. "But I told Danny you would only do it for a ton of money and come on, Becca, we all know you need money. You can't live with your dad forever."

Wow. I had just been put in my place by a child. Great. But she had a point. And I definitely didn't want to seem like a loser in Meredith's eyes. Not that she would ever think of me like that. Or did she?

I was starting to feel sorry for myself again when Dana's voice interrupted my thoughts.

"And how much exactly is a ton of money?" Dana asked, crossing her arms and looking amused. She didn't even try to hide the smile forming on her face.

"Ten thousand to start..."

My mouth fell open. "What? Whhhhhhhhhat?"

Meredith looked smug. "You didn't think I would seriously offer your services and not get you the big bucks, did you? Come on, Becca. I'm way too smart for that."

"I see she's inherited my sense of modesty," Dana said with a laugh.

I was speechless and didn't know how to reply. Ten thousand dollars was a huge chunk of change. There had to be a catch.

"So what's the catch?"

Meredith shook her head and folded her arms across her chest. "I don't know, Becca. I'm just a kid. Danny gave me her number. I'll text it to you and then you can call her and discuss your terms. That is what adults do in business, right?"

I shrugged, but Dana nodded.

"Just don't blow it, okay. I worked really hard to get Danny to convince his aunt that you're awesome enough to do a great job and worth every penny."

I placed my hand over my heart. "I promise I won't mess this up."

"Good." She walked away, and I looked at Dana.

"Wow. She made me feel like a clueless child."

"She does that really well." Dana turned to me and continued, "Ten thousand dollars. Yikes. She must really hate that guy."

I shifted uncomfortably. My stilettos were killing my ankles, but that wasn't the only thing bothering me. "I hope she isn't some sort of micromanaging crazy person." I already had enough of that with Leona.

"Me too."

My phone beeped. I looked down and realized it was from Meredith. Her text just had the number I needed and the name.

I read the name, "Claire Doogan."

"Claire Doogan, that's kind of a corny name. For all the money she's offering you, I would expect her name to be Van der Ville or something."

"As long as she's paying me ten thousand, her name could be Princess Aurora for all I care."

Dana laughed, "My sassiness is finally rubbing off on you. That's what I like to hear."

I laughed and made my way back to my car after I said my goodbyes.

I didn't wait. As soon as I sat in the car and closed the door, I called her.

"This is the Doogans' residence," the voice answered. I was intimidated. With its perfect elocution, I felt like a hick suddenly.

I cleared my throat. "Yes, errr ... my name ... is..." I paused after each word and cleared my throat. I could practically feel the impatience of the person on the other end. I must have sounded so incompetent. Get it together, Becca, I hissed at myself in my head.

This time with what I hoped sounded like self-confidence, I said, "I'm Becca. I was told to call this number to speak to Claire Doogan regarding a personal matter."

"I'll have Mrs. Doogan return your call. Enjoy the

rest of your day." And then, before I could say another word, the call ended.

I sighed, grabbed the steering wheel with both hands, and placed my head on it. I was sure I had just made the best impression in the world.

"Oh well, back to minimum wage," I said forlornly as I guided the car away from the school and toward home.

Home was a very modest, kind of ugly, mustard yellow condo building on the rough side of town. My father had lived there for at least ten years now. The building was kind of rundown and in exchange for rent, my dad did random jobs around the condo for the manager. He was a handyman and sometimes worked retail too when money was tight. Growing up money had always been tight, but I would have rather been poor than live with my mom any day. My mom drove me crazy.

Speaking of which, I hadn't heard from her in about a month. Thank god. No wonder it had been such a great month. I instantly felt bad for thinking that, but decided to harden my heart a little. She didn't deserve person of the year or anything. I wondered about my siblings. We weren't close since they lived so far away, and they were all younger than me. I sent birthday cards and presents when I could, but never heard anything back from them. Sometimes I wondered if my mom even told them about me since she pretended that her first marriage to my father hadn't really happened. And when I had decided to go live with him after their divorce, she had punished me by not speaking to me for years.

I pushed thoughts of my mom away and made my way toward the unit I shared with my dad. I could see a few of my neighbors lounging on their patios, fiddling with their plants or just enjoying the weather. The neighbors were really nice and most had lived here for years. I was greeted by a group of them sitting in white plastic chairs, playing a game of dominos, in the courtyard that sat directly in the center of the condo's outdoor space.

Mrs. Nguyen waved to me and greeted me in Vietnamese. She was determined to teach me her native language, but I had barely learned hello. Languages just weren't my specialty. Honestly, I wasn't too sure what my specialty was. I was still trying to figure out life.

"Hi, Mrs. Nguyen. Isn't it a little too hot outside for you?"

She shook her head. "It's fine. Better the heat than the cold. I hate the cold." She narrowed her eyes at me and said with a voice full of judgment, "Weren't you wearing that the other night? You said you were on your way to work. Exactly what type of work do you do, young lady? You're not one of those sex workers, are ya?" She arched a brow and waited for me to answer.

The others stopped playing dominos and looked toward me waiting for me to confirm probably what they were all suspecting. Great, my neighbors thought I was a prostitute.

I sputtered, "Mrs. Nguyen, of course not. You need to stop watching so much Crime TV."

She shrugged. "No way. I need to know what's really going on in the world." Without another word she turned back to the dominos game along with the others.

I shook my head and heard a laugh near me, "Did Mrs. Nguyen just accuse you of being a prostitute?"

Dad was standing there with the door open. Apparently, he had overheard our conversation. I wasn't surprised. I was sure the whole condo building had heard our conversation.

"Yes. I'm just going to pretend that never happened."

He frowned. "That dress is a little too short."

"Dad," I whined like a teenager, "it was for work."

"Maybe you need to find a different job then. You're a smart girl. There's no need for you to be doing whatever it is you do..." He paused and said, "What is it that you do again?"

I rolled my eyes and made my way into the condo. He closed the door behind me, and I stomped off into my room and changed clothes. It was hot. I didn't know how much more of the heat wave I could survive. August sucked.

I came out to join him at the table where he was busy sorting bills. He frowned as he did.

"Bad news?"

"Bills are always bad news."

He was right about that. We were always on a budget. Money was always tight. I hated checking the mail. I had foolishly taken out student loans for my undergraduate program, and I was kicking myself now for accepting them. I hated debt. I hated not being able to help more with the bills. I felt like I was a burden on my father although I would never tell him that. It would hurt him if he knew I felt that way and since he was my biggest supporter in the world, I would never say or do anything to hurt him.

I sort of felt like it was just me and my dad against the world.

"I should have a check coming in soon," I said with false cheer. "I ran into my boss at Meredith's talent show."

"How was the talent show?" he asked as he looked through the bills, frowning.

"Great," I said, looking at him. His brows were pinched with worry, and I watched as he scratched at his hairline. He was going bald but was too proud to just completely cut off all his hair, so he just had combed over the bald spot with what little hair lined the top of his head. I had tried to get him to cut it all off when he had first started going bald last year, but he had stubbornly refused.

"Some hair is better than no hair," was his mantra. I totally disagreed.

"Dad."

He didn't answer.

"Dad," I said again as he frowned at a bill.

"Huh?" He looked up then.

"Don't get stressed out. We'll take care of this. Okay?"

He gave me a wry smile. "Not we. Me. They're my bills."

"I want to help," I protested, but there was no use. Like I said, he was stubborn. Dad had been hospitalized with pneumonia about two months ago, and because he didn't have insurance the bill had been ridiculous.

We had negotiated the bill down, but we still owed quite a bit. I didn't know what we were going to do. Even though Dad had always been a blue collar worker, he paid all his bills on time, so I knew it was tearing away at him that he couldn't afford to pay his hospital bill.

He sighed and went to the small kitchen and started making lunch.

"What do you think? Mac and cheese?"

I smiled. Mac and cheese was my favorite meal. "Sounds great, Dad."

He started cooking and I watched him, finally noticing that he had aged. His jet black hair now was gray in some places and his eyes had little crinkles around the edges. My dad was getting older, and I needed to step it up. I wasn't going to wait for Claire Doogan to call me. Nope. I needed ten thousand dollars desperately. I was going to call her.

2

"**M**iss, umm ... your card was declined," said the embarrassed barista as he looked at me.

"That's not possible. I swear there's money on here," I argued even though I could see the message myself, "Transaction Denied."

"Let me just try again," I said, impatience entering my voice.

"I'll handle it," Mrs. Doogan said, and I wanted the ground to swallow me up.

"It's okay. I don't need the coffee," I said to her, feeling beyond embarrassed.

I had called her number again and this time the person who answered had been able to connect me with her. Mrs. Doogan had agreed to meet me immediately the next day. To my surprise, she had been really pleasant. She was very likeable and nice. Her butler or whomever answered the phone had been the only jerk, so far.

We were at a posh coffee shop that had been converted from an old residential home. I didn't particularly care for it. It was trendy and a lot of hipsters frequented it. It made me feel like a poser, an imposter. Kind of how I felt when I was married to my ex and he insisted that I go to parties on yachts with him. I had always found myself hiding in the bathroom while he and his friends did all sorts of unsavory things, gratefully, without me. I was a blue collar girl all the way. I wasn't sure why I married Tom. A lapse in judgement, for sure.

So when Mrs. Doogan suggested the place, I had readily agreed. When I arrived, I realized that it was one of "those" places and had instantly felt uncomfortable. To make up for it, I quickly acted like the imposter I was and tried to impress Mrs. Doogan by buying her coffee. That was what I got for not checking my bank account, I thought miserably as Mrs. Doogan bought both our coffees. I wanted to cry. I had wanted to make a good impression; instead, I was doing the exact opposite.

I plastered a determined smile on my face and thanked her as we returned to our small table. I studiously didn't look at anyone else. I didn't know if everyone had seen what had just happened, but I was so embarrassed by it. I felt like everyone was laughing at me.

"Thanks for taking care of the coffees," I said with false cheer. "I guess it's pretty clear, I really do need your money, huh?" I said with a forced chuckle, and then I wanted to kick myself. Why did I just say something THAT stupid?

To my surprise, she laughed. "I don't know," she said, looking down at her coffee. "Six bucks for a cup of joe is rather steep by anyone's standards."

Instantly, my tension melted from my shoulders. Gosh, a few seconds ago, I hadn't even known that I was tense. Mrs. Doogan was a nice lady. Way better than Leona, who until that minute I had forgotten to check in with. Dammit. Leona was going to be pissed. She might even fire me, which was even more motivation to get this job.

"So, Mrs. Doogan—"

"Please, call me Claire."

I smiled. "Claire, and um, please call me Becca," I instantly felt like an idiot again. She had been calling me Becca the whole time. I was such a ditz sometimes. It was amazing that I made it through college.

"Sure, Becca," she said, clearly amused.

"So who's this guy you want me to follow?"

From her purse, she pulled out a phone, and on it were various pictures of the dude. He had a nice smile, was my first thought. He smiled like the world didn't matter. Just really unguarded. The type of smile a girl could fall for. Obviously, he was trouble.

"So this is the rascal?"

She laughed at my word choice. "That's one thing to call him."

She sighed heavily and said, "But yes, this is Julius Romo." She puckered her lips in distaste, sitting back and crossing her hands in her lap. She was wearing cotton shorts that accentuated her long, blemish-free legs. Her legs were even better than mine. She was wearing a salmon-colored blouse with large bell sleeves. She wore her hair up in a simple chignon with dangly earrings.

She looked rich. Something about her screamed money and privilege. Frankly, I wouldn't have been surprised if she was royalty. I could picture people bowing to her. I guessed her to be in her late forties. She was beautiful. Elegant. Well-composed. Everything I would like to grow up to be.

"He plans to marry my daughter in less than two months' time. I know nothing about him besides the basic information." She started to list what she knew about him. "His social security number. Criminal background, which unfortunately was clear. Some basic genetic stuff since I took a DNA sample when he wasn't paying attention."

I tried to look as if it was completely normal to know those things about a future son-in-law. Mrs. Doogan was apparently thorough. So why did she need me?

"So what do you want me to do since you know so much about him already?"

"Follow him around. See where he goes. Who he talks to. See what he's hiding." She gave a frustrated sigh. "My daughter is naive. Sweet. Trusting. Gullible. I love her, but she's like a sheep among wolves. I'm very rich, Becca. And my Ana has been very sheltered. I got to where I am not by being the smartest or working the hardest, but by being tough. And it seems along the way, I didn't show my daughter how to use that same grit to see through lies. So that's why I need your help. I need evidence to convince her to listen to me. I'm not going to have her throw her life away on some random man who may or may not be after her money."

I wondered then if that was how people had seen me when I had married Tom. They had probably thought I was a gold digger too. After all, he had been well-off and I had only been nineteen.

"What makes you think he's after her money? Couldn't he just sign a prenup?"

"Oh, he said he would. I don't believe him. And even if I did, I still wouldn't want her to waste even a second of her life on him. He's not good enough for her. He's below her." She finished with a shake of her head, as if frustrated by the mere thought of him. For the first time, I wondered if I was an accurate judge of character. Maybe Mrs. Doogan wasn't who she had first appeared to be. Maybe she wasn't all that pleasant, after all.

What kind of person would describe someone as being below another? Ouch. Mrs. Doogan or Claire, as she insisted I call her, didn't downplay the fact that she felt superior to others. I wondered if she felt superior to me. I sighed. She probably did; after all, I couldn't even afford two cups of coffee. She was superior to me, at least when finances were concerned. Stupid coffee had made me look bad.

"And you came highly recommended, so I can trust you to be discrete, I'm sure." I wanted to laugh that my recommendation had come from a little boy.

"Danny said you were very pretty, and he was right. You can follow them around and seem like you're part of the background. No one will notice you. You're the perfect age." She leaned in and said, "Now about your fee..."

I winced. "Yes, I know it's a little—"

"Cheap," she finished for me. I looked at her in surprise; I was going to say steep.

"You might be inexpensive, but I trust you. Just get me the info I need. I'm not one of those who believes the old adage 'you get what you pay for.' Take this coffee for example. I don't think it's superior to any regular one dollar coffee that I could get from McDonald's. So yes, I could find a more expensive freelance P.I, or whatever you call yourself, but I trust you can actually get the job done. So can you?" She arched her brow and gave me an inquisitive look. I had to believe in myself. After all, she did.

"I can do it. No problem."

She smiled. "I know you can."

She stood up then and slid on a pair of shades. "Of course, I don't expect you to start without payment. I'll wire the first half to your account within twenty-four hours. And then you'll get the other half after the job is done. You'll receive a contract at your home within the hour. Thanks, Becca. And by the way, he always shows up here around one o'clock."

She checked her watch. "So I guess, you might as well start now."

One o'clock? That was less than ten minutes away, I wanted to say, but Claire had already made a hasty exit through the back.

I noticed then that she had left her phone. I tucked it in my purse to return to her. God, I should have taken notes. What did she say his name was? Julian? Jude? Jonathan? Something Roman? Great. I was off to the worst start.

And then, like clockwork, he walked through the door. He didn't look like every other guy in the place, so

I wasn't the only one who noticed his arrival. While most of the guys in the coffee shop had on fashionable skinny jeans and "iconic" band shirts with little row boats on them, this guy was wearing old khaki shorts with a hole in the pocket and upon further inspection, as he passed by me, I noticed that his plain t-shirt was stained and he was wearing some very ugly sandals.

And despite all that, he was still the best looking man in the place. The pictures hadn't done him justice. He passed by not noticing me, and that felt a little weird. I was used to masculine attention now. I hadn't been ignored by a guy since high school. In fact, it hadn't been until after high school that I had come into my own. In retrospect, that was probably why I had married Tom. He had paid attention to me when I was used to being ignored. Ignored by my peers. Ignored by my mom. But now wasn't the time to think about my failed marriage or my lukewarm relationship with my mom. I had much bigger fish to fry.

He smiled at the barista as he ordered his coffee. He had a great smile, just like in the pictures. His eyes were the lightest blue I had seen and I couldn't help it, as he passed by, I checked out his butt. I was a fan of guys with nice butts, and Julius didn't disappoint. I reminded myself that he was getting married so I needed to not think about his attractiveness. I also had to remind myself that he was a rascal. God, I felt like a heroine in an old romance novel. Who used the word rascal anymore?

He sat a table close by and started sipping his coffee. To my surprise, he didn't pull out a phone like everyone else. Instead, he reached in his back pocket and pulled out a comic book. He placed it gently on the table and started reading it. Every now and then he would let out a bark of laughter. It startled the rest of the customers who looked "too cool" to laugh. I liked his smile, and I felt his laughter was contagious. Every time he laughed, I couldn't help but smile. My coffee was getting cold, and I knew I should head out so that he wouldn't notice me, but I awkwardly didn't know where to start. I wasn't a P.I. I was just the girl who followed people around and took pictures.

I awkwardly sat there trying to come up with a plan when my phone rang. I looked down and realized it was Leona. I knew if I ignored it she would probably come to my house and try to murder me, so instead I answered.

"Hi," I whispered.

"Hello ... hello. Helllllloooooooooooooooooo," she said impatiently. Clearly, she hadn't heard me answer.

"Hi," I said a little louder, turning away from Julius.

"Where the hell are my pictures? I did not hire you to do nothing! I want those pictures..." To my horror, I had accidentally hit the speakerphone setting so everyone in the small, cozy coffee house could clearly hear me being yelled at by Leona.

I fumbled to take the speakerphone setting off and finally was victorious. I received a few looks and ignored the eyes of the patrons, one of which was Julius. He looked bemused.

"Uh, yeah. I'm so, so, so sorry. I just got caught up."

"Caught up? I don't pay you to get caught up. I pay you to take pictures and deliver them to me. So how about you do that?"

"Yes," I stuttered, "Of course, Leona. I'm on it. No problem."

She hung up abruptly, and I sat back and sighed, avoiding the looks from other onlookers who I was sure still heard part of Leona's tirade. After all, she had been yelling.

I bit my lip, trying to figure out what to do next when Julius stood up, tucked his comic in his back pocket, and walked over to me.

I didn't know what to say or do, so I just sat there like a deer caught in headlights. My brain told me to run and hide, but my brain was stupid. That was a terrible plan.

"Hi," he said.

"Hi," I mumbled back.

"Can I sit down?"

"Ummm sure," I said, looking left and right. I was

caught. He caught me. I was only on the job for ten minutes and he already caught me. I was a failure. So stupid. So, so stupi—

"My name's Julius, and I'm looking for a photographer. I couldn't help but overhear your conversation."

"My conversation?" I sounded like an idiot and felt like one again.

"The conversation between you and the yelling woman. About photos? You are a photographer, right?" I could hear the words coming out of his mouth, but my brain hadn't caught up yet. Did he know who I was? What was happening here? Was he trying to hire me? I couldn't take all the questions. Too much for one day, so I answered the easiest one first.

"Um, yes. Yes, I am. A photographer. Yes."

He smiled. "Great, I almost felt really stupid for a second."

I smiled then. "I know the feeling..."

Our eyes held as we sat smiling at each other when I remembered that he was a rascal. I wasn't supposed to be staring in his eyes. I was supposed to be following him around.

Well, I had blown that, so I had to try something else.

"So you were saying you need a photographer? For what exactly?"

He paused then and seemed to blush. He raked a

hand through his hair and laughed as he said, "My wedding, actually."

"Oh," I pretended to be surprised. "You're getting married? How soon? I mean, I need to know if I can fit you in my schedule." Good save.

"Um … like in a month or two?"

I tried to not sound suspicious as I said as indifferently as possible, "A month or two? You don't know when you're getting married?"

"Well, there have been some complications…"

"Uh oh, starting to get cold feet?"

"What? No… I just…."

"You … just … what?"

"Nothing. It's complicated. But like I said, I'm looking for a photographer, and I would love to see your work."

He reached into his back pocket and took out a card. He handed it to me. "Email me your portfolio, and I'll take a look."

Portfolio? Did I even have a portfolio? Only if he wanted a bunch of pictures of cheating spouses getting blowjobs from complete strangers or exes. Jeez, my job made me feel dirty. But wedding photography, now that sounded pleasant. And I could kill two birds with one stone. I could follow him around, earn ten thousand dollars, and build a respectable portfolio. That sounded like a win-win to me. First, I needed to get him to hire me. I was sure he came over to meet me because he felt sorry for me. That was okay. I felt sorry for me too.

"Thanks. I'll do that. Thanks so much."

He got up and walked away. I watched his butt as he did and then he abruptly turned around. I promptly raised my eyes and hoped he hadn't caught me. He walked back to me. Oh no, I was in trouble.

"I didn't get your name."

"Oh," I said, caught off guard. "Becca," I extended my hand, "I'm Becca."

"Becca," he said, taking my hand just long enough for me to feel the calluses on his palm. It seemed Julius worked for a living. "I look forward to seeing your work."

He let go of my hand, gave me a brief smile, and walked away. So far, Julius had been a complete gentleman. I didn't think he was a rascal, but time would tell. After all, I was being paid ten thousand dollars just to prove he wasn't the man he seemed to be.

3

"So let me get this right," Dana said, sitting next to me on Piper's couch. Piper was Tom's sister, which made her my former sister-in-law. But now we were all friends. And as her friend, she had roped me into house-sitting for her for a few weeks. She was in Europe house hunting with her husband, Ty. They were looking for a vacation home somewhere in Italy, or was it France? I couldn't remember. "You met the guy who you're supposed to be following, and he offered to hire you?"

"Yeah, that's exactly what happened."

"And that wasn't part of the plan. Right?"

"Well..."

Dana shot me a dubious look, and I sighed. "Okay. No. That wasn't part of the plan, but maybe it'll work out for the best."

Dana continued to look doubtful, and I tried not to feel discouraged, but I did. What the heck was I doing?

"You think I messed up, don't you?"

She opened her mouth to respond, took one look at my face and seemed to second guess herself. "I'm sure it'll be fine."

Her face told a different story. She was humoring me. She thought I had already failed, and I hadn't even started. I suddenly felt so discouraged. "I hope so." I shook my head. "I just don't know what I'm doing anymore. I'm a mess. My life is a mess."

"Woah, where is all this coming from? You haven't even started the job yet."

"I know. I think I just bit off more than I could chew."

"I'm sure you'll do fine."

"Your face says exactly the opposite."

"My face is stupid and never does what I tell it."

I giggled, and then Dana started laughing too. I really valued Dana's friendship. And I knew she wasn't trying to be a Debbie Downer, but she couldn't help herself.

When we stopped laughing, she offered up some advice. "You should probably tell your employer what your plan is so she's not shocked to see you at the wedding."

"Well, if I do my job there will be no wedding."

"True. So what's your plan?"

"Well," I said, "first of all, I need you to make me a portfolio."

"What? Me?"

"Yeah ... you have computer skills."

"Umm, but not Photoshop or whatever. I do marketing."

"That's sort of the same."

"No, actually, it's not. Not even close."

I sighed. "Then what am I going to do?" I felt like I was back to square one again. "I don't have a portfolio to show this guy, but I have to land this job otherwise I can't follow him around because then he'll recognize me and know I'm up to no good," I whined.

"Calm down. We'll figure this out. I might know someone who can help."

I grabbed her hands and bounced up and down in excitement. "Oh my gosh, thank you, thank you, thank you..."

"Okay, okay." She pried her hands away and laughed. "I said might, so we'll see. I'll give him a call. I can't believe I'm going to ask someone to create a fake portfolio for you. Next thing you know I'll be in the business of making fake passports and stuff."

"I'm sure making a fake portfolio isn't like some sort of gateway drug to criminal activity."

"Good one," she said, punching my shoulder. "My sense of humor is rubbing off on you."

"Yep."

"That means you spend too much time with me. You need to get out more. Any luck finding a boyfriend yet?"

Gosh, sometimes Dana was like an annoying big sister. "Not looking for one."

"Come on, you're young and hot ... all the things I used to be."

I snorted, and she continued with a smile on her face, "I'm serious. You need to get out there. Find a man. Fall in love. Have some babies."

"Nope. I'm fine. Being single suits me."

"Well, at least hook-up with some randos, you know, and really enjoy your youth."

"You only slept with Tom and Carter," I said holding back laughter.

"I know. And Carter has even more moves than he did in college. Like seriously, sometimes the sex is so good it makes my head hurt."

I couldn't hold back my laughter even though I knew I was probably blushing. I never knew what Dana was going to say next. She then frowned and said, "And let's be honest, Tom wasn't exactly lightning in bed."

"What? Are you kidding me? He was like lightning..." I paused for dramatic effect, "...he came quickly."

She let out a bark of laughter and said, "And then snored like thunder minutes later."

We collapsed in laughter while squealing, "Lightning and thunder," like a couple of teenagers.

When we were ready to behave like adults again, Dana got up and called in that favor then we sat around and started watching a movie. Carter had gone to some sort of conference, and the kids were staying overnight at Carter's mom's house, so it was officially a girls' night for us.

We were in the middle of a romantic comedy that included a bride running away from the altar whose acting skills Dana happily criticized.

"There's something about her face I just don't like," Dana said with a serious look on her face. "You know what I mean?"

I shrugged. "I think she's pretty."

"You say that about everyone."

"No, I don't."

"Yes, you do. You're all sugar and spice and everything nice."

"Hey, you're nice too."

She shot me a pointed look, and I mumbled, "Well, mostly nice."

I continued, "What did your friend say?"

"Oh yeah, he'll do it."

I squealed and went to hug her again. I grabbed around her neck while saying "Thank you, thank you," over and over, and she pried at my arms.

"I can't breathe," she hissed.

"Oh, sorry." I promptly put my arms down.

"So when will he be done?"

"Like an hour."

"Wow."

"Yeah, and he's going to build you a website too. It's going to be awesome."

"All that in an hour?"

"The dude doesn't have a life."

"I'm surprised you're not trying to convince me to date him."

"I want you to date someone fun. I love Mac, but he's like the opposite of fun."

"At least you have standards for me."

"Yeah, anyone who is not a loser and not Tom."

"Thanks."

"No problem."

"Literally, an hour later we were sitting in front of the computer looking at my "portfolio."

"He did a great job. Tell Mac I said thank you."

"Will do." She gave a big yawn and stood up. "I'm heading home. I'm exhausted."

"It's eight-thirty."

"Oh good. I can sleep for ten hours at least before I have to pick Carter up from the airport. See you later. Tell me if you need anything."

When she was gone, I sent an email to Julius.

I sat in front of the TV and continued checking my email. I had one from my mom accusing me of avoiding her calls. I was surprised until she mentioned that she had a new number. I screened all my calls, so I didn't pick up numbers I didn't recognize. I knew she wanted me to feel guilty, but I refused. Whatever. She should have told me earlier that she had a new number. But I couldn't stay hard-hearted for more than a few minutes. I emailed her back. To my credit, I didn't apologize. I just told her that I hadn't known she'd changed her number.

I called my dad to check on him. He promptly informed me that mom had texted him and accused him of turning me against her. Typical Mom.

I reassured him that I had reached out to her, and then I checked my email again. To my surprise, I had a reply from Julius.

Nervously, I clicked on it. It was a short message:

Portfolio looks great. You're hired. We'll be in touch.

J-

I CALLED CLAIRE, and she promptly picked up. "Call me from the burner phone," she said and then hung up.

"Burner phone?" What was she, a spy or something? And what was the burner phone? Then I remembered the phone she had left on the table. Claire was something else, that's for sure.

I pulled the phone from my purse and called her number which I realized was already programmed into the phone.

"Okay, so what did you think? Did you stake him out?"

"Better than that," I said with fake confidence. "I convinced him to hire me as the wedding photographer."

She was silent for a long time and then said, "Forgive me if I'm misunderstanding, but wasn't your job to make sure there isn't a wedding?"

I was immediately intimidated by the anger in her voice and was so happy we were having this conversation over the phone instead of face-to-face. Claire was tough.

I tried to keep my voice from shaking as I replied. "I plan to make sure a wedding definitely doesn't happen. My plan is to freely follow him around with my camera now that I have a reason to be around."

"Hmmm... That plan might work. At least it better, or you're going to be out ten thousand dollars."

She was threatening me. That didn't feel too good. I swallowed hard. I was determined not to show her that I was as clueless as I sounded.

"Trust me, Claire, I've done this type of thing before.

This is my expertise," I lied, hoping I sounded convincing.

"Okay. Just get results." She paused for a second and said, "Actually, I think this arrangement might work to my advantage. I'll arrange an engagement event or two. You're bound to catch him showing his true colors eventually. This was actually a great plan, Becca. We'll be in touch. Have a great evening."

I hung up feeling vindicated. And then my phone beeped with an incoming text. From my bank.. A wire transfer for $5000 was scheduled for tomorrow.

I jumped up and down squealing in joy and then made myself sit down and be quiet. I didn't want any of Piper's neighbors calling the cops on me for disturbing the peace.

That night I went to bed with a smile on my face. And people said money didn't buy happiness.

I HEARD from Julius the next day. Again, by email. He told me that his future mother-in-law had planned some sort of impromptu engagement party, and he wanted to know if I would be available to take pictures this upcoming weekend. I said yes, of course, and then texted Claire that I would be arriving.

She texted back: *Ha. I'm a mastermind. See you there.*

I was feeling pretty good. If I used Twitter, I would have posted something about it. But since I didn't use social media, I did a happy dance instead.

I spent the rest of the week taking care of minor jobs for Leona. I was tempted to quit because of the five thousand dollar advance, but I didn't want to seem like a flake. People didn't take me seriously because of my beauty and they assumed I was a spoiled Disney princess, and sure, I'd made some stupid mistakes in my life, but I was determined to prove them wrong. I wasn't a quitter. The only thing I ever quit in life was my marriage, but that had been for survival. I felt like I had been losing myself while married to Tom. In fact, when I had married him I didn't even know who I was. I was happy that I was able to figure it out. Well, I hadn't actually figured it out. I had just moved on.

I wasn't too sure what people wore to engagement parties. I'd had one, but it had been on Tom's friend's yacht and I spent most of the party with my head in a toilet bowl. Seasickness had been an issue until Tom introduced me to Dramamine. So I didn't remember what my guests had worn. And to be honest, the guests had been Tom's friends. I didn't have many friends then, and I didn't have many now. Thankfully though, I had Piper and Dana now in my life.

I decided on a yellow and white striped dress. I slid on some flats and hoped that my hair would dry on the way. I was already running late and didn't have time to blow-dry it. I jumped in my car, which had just had a tune up courtesy of Claire's advance, and sped to the engagement party.

I arrived at a place that I remembered used to be a club when I was a teenager. Now it was a trendy outdoor/indoor event area. I was surprised Claire chose this as a location. It seemed sort of out of character. Like it just wasn't classy enough. And it seemed unnecessarily large.

I pulled up to the front, and a valet approached me. I didn't want to pay a valet anything.

"It's free, ma'am," he said. I guessed he could tell from my face that I was cheap.

I thanked him and asked where I could find the Doogan family.

"Just inside..." he said as I handed him my keys. "They rented the whole building for the event."

I was in shock. The whole building? Wouldn't a room or two be a better idea? Rich people were like a different species as far as I was concerned.

As soon as I entered, I easily spotted Claire. She was in a corner on the lawn talking to a young lady with short curly hair who was wearing ill-fitting slacks and a short jacket. I figured the lady in the slacks was some sort of event planner. She hurriedly walked away from

Claire who turned and walked away from the event completely.

The young lady in the slacks stopped and spoke to a girl who was about my age. I figured the woman she was speaking to was the bride because of the way the event planner seemed to fuss over her.

The bride was redheaded and had flawless pale skin. Her lips were painted a dark red and when she turned in my direction, I saw that her eyes were a really light brown. In short, she was beautiful. She looked like an ice queen, but her eyes radiated warmth.

She smiled timidly at me as I approached and said, "Hi, welcome. You must be a friend of Julius?"

I nodded and extended my hand; she shook it.

"She's the photographer I told you about," Julius said, appearing from seemingly nowhere.

"Ana, this is Rebecca, Rebecca, this is Ana."

My name was actually just Becca, but I didn't bother to correct him.

"It's nice to meet you, Ana. Thanks for hiring me."

She pointed at Julius. "He's handling all the wedding stuff. I'm afraid that weddings just aren't my thing, so you just have Julius to thank. He had nothing but nice things to say about you. And what I saw of your portfolio, I really liked."

"Thanks," I murmured, feeling embarrassed by the

compliments and also embarrassed that my whole portfolio was just a lie.

Lying was not my forte.

Ana introduced me to the wedding planner, and I tried not to notice how handsome Julius looked. He was wearing jeans much to my surprise and a plain blue shirt. Not that his casual wear didn't make him look great. Again, he was hands down the best looking guy there. I felt guilty thinking that and quickly directed my attention elsewhere.

"Come meet my mother," Ana said with clear reluctance. "I'm sure she has some photo ideas she would like to share with you."

"Better yet. Hey, Julius, I need to speak to the event planner. Can you take Rebecca to meet Mom?"

He shook his head. "Nope. No thank you. You handle your mother, that's our agreement."

They stared each other down for a second, and I smelled trouble in paradise. Julius lost the stare down and reluctantly told me to follow him.

"You owe me big time," he retorted to Ana.

"I know, I know," she said, looking perturbed but also relieved. Was Ana afraid of her own mother?

"Come on, come meet the Dragon Lady."

"Julius..."

I could hear the warning in Ana's voice.

"What? I mean that in the most complimentary way. Trust me."

I didn't trust a word he said, but he made me laugh.

"Dragon lady?" I said when we were out of earshot. "I'm guessing she doesn't know you call her that."

He laughed, "Are you kidding me? I value my life."

I laughed, "She can't be that bad."

"You're right. She's a million times worse."

I couldn't tell if he was joking or not. So I guessed the feeling was mutual. They hated each other.

"Claire," he called as we crossed the lawn.

I knew she could hear us, but she blatantly ignored Julius.

"Claire," he called again.

She looked away from whomever she was talking to on the phone and said, "Were you raised in a barn? Stop shouting at me."

"I'm not shouting. I was just trying to get your attention."

"Well now you have it. What do you want?"

Yikes, she hated him.

"This is Rebecca," he said tightly. "Rebecca, this is Claire Doogan. Annie's mom."

"Ana, her name is Ana. Annie sounds so juvenile."

Yikes, again.

"So, Rebecca, is it?"

I shrugged and decided to go with it. It would be better if he didn't really know my name.

"So, Rebecca, you're the what exactly?"

"Photographer I hired."

"Well since Julius hired you, I'm hoping you're at least somewhat competent."

Ouch. I hoped she didn't mean that. Hopefully, she was just really trying to sell the role.

Julius' voice was tight and controlled as he said carefully, "I can assure you that Ms. Rebecca is very good at her job. One of the best. And I'm sure you have plenty of photo ideas to discuss with her, so I'll leave you guys to it."

He walked away without another word, and Claire stared at him as he made his way across the lawn and disappeared into the building.

I could see in her eyes that if he suddenly died right then and there she would throw an even bigger party in celebration.

She turned to me. "Sorry for being such a bitch." I was surprised she was so self-aware.

"He brings out the worst in me. I hate his guts. But don't worry. The feeling's mutual. I've disliked him since the moment I met him."

"How long have they known each other?" I asked, trying to stick to a safer subject.

She shrugged. "I don't know. They met through a mutual friend. Some guy named Sam. Why couldn't she just meet someone in college like every other girl? A future engineer or a doctor would have been nice. Is that really too much to ask? Not that she went to a good college anyway. I tried my best to get her to go to an Ivy League. Brown at the very least, but she insisted on going to a state school. I think she did it to spite me. Who does that?"

She would be absolutely horrified if I told her that not only had I gone to a public university, but I had also gone to a community college before that.

I didn't answer her question because I figured it was rhetorical, but she was still talking anyway.

"And then, she wanted to be a music major. A music major? That's not a real major unless you want to live the rest of your life in poverty." Claire shuddered as if the mere thought of poverty made her ill. "She has terrible judgement. And no matter how hard I try she just doesn't listen to me. Why of all the men in the world would she want to marry him? Him?!"

Okay, now we were back to talking about Julius. I shrugged. I still wasn't sure what was so bad about Julius.

"If you don't mind me asking, why do you dislike him so much?"

She laughed humorless and said, "Becca, I could make you a list that stretches around the whole block;

instead, how about just the highlights? I hate that he doesn't have a job."

"He doesn't?"

"He does something on social media. Sits around on his computer all day. That's not a job. That's a hobby."

I didn't dare tell her that plenty of people made their income through social media. Good incomes at that. But I was sure she didn't want to hear that, so I just listened.

"He always shows me little respect. I know he calls me Dragon Lady behind my back."

I kept my mouth closed. I wasn't going to confirm or deny that.

"And he's just not right for my daughter. She doesn't look happy with him. I mean, look at her. Is that the face of a happy bride-to-be?"

I looked in the direction of Annie—Ana— who was sitting staring at her toes. She didn't look happy, no, not at all.

"Maybe it's just all the wedding stress."

She shrugged. "No, she's looked unhappy for a while now."

"Maybe you should talk to her about it. Maybe there's something else going on in her life that's got her down."

Claire looked sad. "I tried. But it's like she shuts me out on purpose. She doesn't let me in anymore." I could hear the vulnerability in Claire's voice and wanted to reach out and hug her. She sounded like she needed a hug, but then her vulnerable expression was gone and steely anger replaced it. I was glad I hadn't given her hug; she probably would have responded by punching me.

"Anyway, she's unhappy and if he isn't part of the solution, he's part of the problem. He's YOUR problem," she said, turning her fiery eyes back to me. "Find some dirt on him. I'm not going to have him ruin my daughter's life. He makes her unhappy, so he needs to go. I'm counting on you to make sure he does."

"Yes, ma'am," I murmured to the air since she had promptly turned away from me and walked away to greet an older couple who had just arrived.

I remembered then that I was supposed to be photographing the event, so I went back to my car and got my camera. I randomly took pictures of anything and everything. During that time I kept Julius within sight.

He was greeting the guests, and I had to admit, he didn't look all that excited about the engagement party either. I realized in my attempt to find him, I had lost Ana.

I found her next to a fountain at least fifty feet behind the building. It was quiet there, and the busyness of the engagement party seemed miles away. She had taken her heels off and was resting her feet.

"Hi," I said softly, coming to stand next to her.

She smiled up at me. "Hi, how are the festivities going?"

"Everyone is having a good time it seems."

She nodded. "I'm sure they are."

"So," I said, not sure how to bridge the topic, "what are you doing out here? Not a fan of crowds?"

She gestured for me to sit down, and I did.

"I guess you can say that. How do you like being a photographer? I've always wanted to do something creative."

"What do you do now?"

"I work at an accounting firm."

"Oh, you're an accountant?"

"No, I just answer the phone."

"Oh..."

She laughed. "Yeah, I'm twenty-four and still a recep-tionist. I make Mom very proud. That's what I get for going to a state school, as she would say."

She knew her mom well. "I went to a state school."

"Oh, I wasn't trying to say there's anything wrong with them, it's just my mother—"

"Wanted you to go to an Ivy League?"

"Yep. She was so disappointed when I didn't get into Harvard, or Yale, or Stanford, and I didn't even consider applying to Columbia. New York City is too big. I would get lost there, even more lost than I am here."

Her voice trailed off, and I had a feeling that she didn't mean lost just in a directional sense. I sensed there was a lot more emotionally that she wasn't discussing. My heart went out to her. I knew what it felt like to be lost in life. I had felt that way and, to be honest, some days I still did. I couldn't imagine what it would be like to have so many high expectations and not be able to meet them.

My own mother was a force to be reckoned with, but she was hundreds of miles away. And I had my dad who was a sweetheart. Who did Ana have besides the dragon lady? Oh, that was right, she had a knight in shining armor and just like that he showed up.

"What are you ladies doing here all by yourselves; you're missing a fantastic party," he said, taking his shoes off and sitting next to her at the fountain. He stuck his feet in the water and wrapped an arm around her waist.

He placed a kiss on her forehead and said, "Your mom's going to flip out on me if you don't cheer up and at least pretend to be excited."

"There are too many people," Ana said softly. "I hate crowds."

I nodded. "But at least they're friends, right?"

She laughed and I smiled, not sure of the joke.

"They're my mom's friends. Not mine. Definitely not mine."

"Oh, I get it. At my engagement party, it was just my husband's friends, and I puked the entire time."

"So you're married?" Julius asked in surprise, looking at my hand.

"Was. Was married. Long since divorced."

Ana looked at me in surprise. "Seriously, but you must be like my age. How old were you when you got married—eighteen, nineteen?"

"Yep."

"You poor thing," Ana said, and I couldn't help but laugh.

"It wasn't the best relationship to say the least."

"Well, at least you're out of it."

"Yeah, it was one of the smartest decisions I ever made in my life."

"Did you love him?" Ana asked.

I didn't know how to answer her. Had I loved Tom? I thought at the time that I had. Now I wasn't too sure.

So I answered honestly. "I thought I did, when I said yes, but now I think I was just kind of lonely."

"I know what that feels like."

I didn't know how to respond so I said nothing.

Julius, on the other hand, was prepared. He pulled her to his side, like a guardian angel, and they smiled at each other. The love between them was clear. I looked away, not wanting to interrupt a special moment, and then remembering that I was a photographer I stood up and said, "Sorry to interrupt, but hold that pose."

I took the picture and smiled. It was a good one, even I knew that, and I was far from an experienced photographer. I mean I guess I was experienced... I took lots of pictures of cheating spouses. That must have counted for something.

"Ana!" I could hear someone calling from afar and quickly, they both moved to get their feet out of the fountain. That was too bad, I felt it would have made for a really cute picture that they would admire for years to come. Oh yeah, I didn't want them to admire anything for years to come because it was my job to make sure they didn't have a happily ever after.

It was a little old man. "Hi, Grandpa G," Ana said, getting up with a real smile on her face. I took pictures as she crossed over to him. He took her hand and pulled her toward the party.

"Come on, you guys," he said, giving us a warm smile. "Your uncle is about to do a toast, Ana."

Ana and her grandfather walked ahead of us. Something he said made her laugh, and her laugh was contagious. I found myself smiling at the sound of it. She needed to laugh more.

They disappeared around the shrubs, and Julius and I followed behind them.

"So that's Claire's father?"

"No, he's my grandfather."

"Ohhhh…"

"My whole family adores Annie."

"I can see why; just by interacting with her for a few moments, she's a sweet person."

"One of the best," he said. "Just authentic. Down to earth. A genuinely good person. Which makes me convinced that she was adopted."

I looked at him and we both laughed. I knew he was referring to Claire.

"Claire's not so bad."

"That's because you haven't had to spend more than a few moments with her."

I shrugged. "I don't know. She's probably just a concerned mom."

"Concerned that a guy like me is marrying her daughter?" He seemed to take it personal, but I could understand that.

"Maybe it's not you personally."

He shot me a dubious look, and I shrugged.

"Oh, I'm very sure it's personal. She's hated me since she met me."

"Well, maybe she has a reason for hating you?"

"Sure. Because I'm breathing, that's enough for her."

"Well, have you tried just holding your breath around her?" I said, joking to lighten the mood.

"And passing out and dying?"

"Hmmm ... well you do want her approval, right?"

"Sure, I would just rather be alive to get it."

"I'm not sure that will happen."

"You think if I died right here and now that she would just push my body into a dumpster and call it a day."

I shook my head. "I kind of think she would have a party."

He laughed, "You're right."

He paused then and said, "I like your sense of humor, Becca." He squeezed my arm, gave me a brilliant smile, and said, "See you inside."

He had gotten my name right.

I watched as he jogged up the steps and went to stand by Ana's side. She looked up at him with a sense of relief, and he took her hand in hers, giving her a reassuring smile.

I knew I looked weird staring at him, so I took a picture to capture the moment. He was her knight in shining armor. He was her support.

I envied them. I envied Ana, that she had a man like Julius. He was strong, funny, and handsome. Everything a girl could want in a man, and he was completely dedicated to her.

I felt an ache in my heart and chalked it up to loneliness. But as I watched Ana and Julius together, I wished

I had met him first. If nothing else, but to at least be his friend.

4

"So how was the wedding?" my dad asked when I got home that evening.

"It wasn't a wedding, just the engagement party,"

"Oh, well, engagement party then. How was it? Hope it was better than yours. You threw up the whole time."

I had forgotten Dad had been there. "You remember that?"

"Remember that? I was the one who drove to Walgreens to get you Dramamine."

I frowned. "I thought—"

He raised an eyebrow. "That Tom had gotten it?" He shook his head. "He was too busy showing the yacht off to his friends."

Of course, that sounded like him. It seemed even when I knew the worst, I was still trying to see the best in him. I was glad I had wised up and moved on.

"Hey Dad," I said, wondering something I hadn't dared ask.

"Huh, hon?"

"Were you and Mom ever friends?"

He let out a low whistle. "We were a lot of things, but friends definitely wasn't one of them."

I nodded while I digested what he had just said. "Tom and I had been a lot of things too, but never friends."

I bent down and kissed him on the forehead. "Have a good night."

"Heading to bed already?" He had cards in his hand and was shuffling them. "How about a game of poker before bed?"

I was about to decline, but figured, why not? The night was still young.

I finally made it to bed at one in the morning. Dad could play poker all day if I let him.

As I went to sleep, all I could think about was whether or not I would turn into my dad. I knew he was happy, but wasn't he lonely? I didn't think about it often, but if someone had asked me the answer would be yes.

"Please, please take my place," Ana begged me the next day. I was at her apartment, and we were waiting for Julius to show up. She told me it was a wedding emergency and that she needed my help immediately. I dropped what I was doing and headed straight over.

Her apartment was sort of bare, and something about it seemed kind of masculine. I guessed it was the pile of athletic sneakers that were in front of the closet door and the random jerseys thrown across the couch. I was pretty sure Julius didn't live there too, but I guessed he tended to leave his stuff at her place. That made sense. After all, they were engaged.

I looked at her in confusion. What exactly did she want from me? "Take your place for what?"

"I hate flowers. Like I really do...."

"Okay???"

"So can you go pick out flowers with Julius?"

I looked around as if hoping someone could save me, but there were only the two of us there.

"Can't your mom go with him instead?"

She looked at me as if I had lost it. Maybe I had.

"Are you kidding me? Just in case you haven't noticed, they hate each other. If I send my mom and Julius to the floral shop together, neither one will make it out alive."

She had a point, but still, I didn't want to be the sacrificial lamb. I thought about it. It would be a good opportunity to get to know Julius better. Maybe then I could see if he had any skeletons in the closet.

Reluctantly, I said, "Umm... I guess I can do it. Just tell me when."

"Now."

"Now?"

"Thanks so much, I'll tell Julius."

She reached for her phone and started texting him. I felt uncertain. I knew nothing about flowers. Like nothing. My nose felt itchy just thinking about them.

I sat on the couch with her and waited for Julius to respond.

"He'll be here in a few minutes," she reassured me.

We sat there awkwardly, both of us not knowing what else to say to each other.

"Sooo…" I said, tired of the silence, "…how long have you two known each other?"

"We've been friends for a while," she said. "We actually met through a mutual friend."

"Oh, that's nice."

She nodded but didn't add anything. I guessed Ana wasn't much of a conversationalist. I wasn't either, but I tried to find something to talk about to fill the silence.

"So what are you into, Ana?"

"Horses. I used to ride all the time when I was little."

Her answer surprised me. I didn't know anyone who rode horses. "Cool. I've always been afraid of horses. Their big teeth give me the creeps."

She smiled. "They're pretty gentle. I mean, I've been thrown by a spooked horse before, but I didn't get hurt too badly. What about you? What are you into?"

"Sleeping."

We both laughed, and then she said, "What made you get into photography? That's a really interesting hobby."

"It might sound lame, but I like taking pictures of beautiful things."

"That doesn't sound lame."

"Well, it's not as cool as riding horses or"—my eyes drifted to the motorcycle helmet sitting on the counter —"riding a motorcycle. Is that your helmet? Do you ride motorcycles, Ana?"

Her face changed. Gone was her easy smile, and her expression became guarded. "No. Not anymore."

I didn't know what I had said or done wrong, but it was clear that I had made her uncomfortable. I opened my mouth to apologize when I heard a knock at the door.

Ana rushed over to open it, and a smiling Julius came in.

"What's wrong?" he asked, his smile falling as he got a look of Ana's face.

"Oh, nothing. Just tired."

He seemed like he wanted to argue, but then he caught sight of me.

He looked from me to Ana. "You sure you're okay?"

"Fine," she said. "I think I just need some rest."

The look on his face said he didn't believe her, but he didn't argue.

He turned to me. "So I heard you got roped into

looking at flowers with me. Are you going to charge me extra?"

"I should…" I mumbled.

He laughed, "You look so miserable. I think you might actually hate this more than I do."

"That's about right."

We said goodbyes to Ana then made our way to the small parking lot outside of her apartment complex.

"Mind if I drive?"

I shook my head and followed him to his car and tried not to think of how good he smelled as he held the door open for me.

I couldn't help myself as I sniffed the air.

"You okay?" he asked.

"Fine, fine." I awkwardly slid down in the seat, as if I could avoid embarrassment by making myself smaller.

"So how's it going so far?"

"Great."

"Yeah"—he glanced in my direction as he pulled off—"my future mother-in-law isn't diving you crazy?"

"Not yet."

"Give her time."

I laughed, and he smiled at me. I liked the way his lips curved. Oops. I totally shouldn't have been looking at his lips.

He smiled wider then, and I looked elsewhere and

cleared my throat. Oh no. Had he caught me staring at his lips? What the heck was wrong with me?

"So… umm… what kind of flowers do you like?" Stupid question. He was a guy. He just liked football and money. Gosh, I sounded like such a female chauvinist.

"Hmm… I have to admit, I'm partial to gladiolas and birds-of-paradise, but those aren't exactly wedding appropriate flowers."

I frowned. I didn't know much about flowers, but birds-of-paradise didn't sound like a real thing. Maybe he was pulling my leg.

"Haha," I said.

"You know they're a real flower, right?"

"Sure. Now you're just trying to show off."

He laughed, and I tried not to think of how much I liked the sound of it.

"Floral shop, here we come. So tell me about yourself, Becca."

"Um…" What to say? What to say? Two truths and a lie sounded like a good approach. "I'm divorced. I like tacos, and I've never dieted in my life."

Jeez. What was wrong with me? Tacos? Divorced? Dieting? Why did I mention that? And why was I talking about dieting of all things. And I hated tacos. I couldn't eat them without getting messy, so I didn't technically hate them. I loved them. But they sucked to eat.

"Hmm… out of all the things you said I have to take exception to the tacos. Tacos are delicious."

"They are," I conceded, "but then when you end up with taco sauce down your blouse it's not so cute."

"Gosh, I hate when taco sauce gets down my blouse. Especially the spicy sauce."

I laughed. He was funny.

"But seriously," he said, "tell me something about yourself. Something that other people don't know."

I thought hard about it. I might as well tell him the truth. Telling the truth wouldn't blow my cover.

"When I was a little girl, I wanted to be a puppy when I grew up."

He laughed, and I smiled.

"It was kind of ridiculous, and I honestly don't remember it. But my mom says that whenever anyone asked me what I wanted to be, I said a puppy."

"At least you thought outside the box. So are you disappointed?" he said, turning to me as he pulled up to a stoplight. I looked at him then. His eyes were warm, unguarded, and I felt mesmerized by them. I had his full attention and, like an idiot, I couldn't get a word out. What had he just asked me? Oh, yeah, he asked me if I was disappointed.

"Disappointed by what?" I asked, still staring at him.

"Disappointed by turning into a beautiful, interesting woman instead of a puppy."

I looked away and knew I was blushing. Had he just called me beautiful?

I shrugged and tried to play it cool. "I don't know," I said, looking away, "being a person instead of a dog definitely has its perks."

He laughed, and a horn sounded behind us.

"What's up with that bozo?" he asked, looking into the rearview mirror.

"Umm… it's a green light," I said, pointing.

He accelerated, and the man behind us sped up and gave us the finger, while yelling out an obscenity.

"Hope you have a great day too!" Julius yelled back.

I giggled. Julius was fun.

"You know what's wrong with the world today, Becca?"

I shook my head.

"Common decency. People just don't have a sense of common decency anymore."

I smiled. "You sound like my father."

"Your father must be a very great, wise, force of a man."

My smile widened. "Yeah… exactly. He's all those things."

Julius chuckled.

We settled into comfortable silence, and I couldn't help but be curious about him. Would it be so bad to ask him a personal question? Maybe it would help me figure out what made him tick.

"So what about you?"

"What about me?" he said, pulling up to the florist shop.

"Tell me something about you that most people don't know."

He parked the car and unbuckled his seatbelt.

"Well, I never wanted to be a puppy; I was a much more realistic child."

I playfully punched him in the shoulder, and he pretended it hurt.

"Ouch."

"Whatever."

"Come on. Tell me."

He shrugged. "I can't think of anything." And then he turned toward me and met my eyes. He smiled.

"You look like the adult version of a cherub in a Renaissance painting."

I crossed my arms. "Was that supposed to distract me? Answer the question."

"Okay. Here's a doozey. Are you ready for this?"

I nodded. Practically salivating. Oh, this was going to be good.

"I..." he stopped. "I... are you sure you want to know?"

I sighed and gave him what I hoped was a mean look.

"Now you look like a mean cherub."

"Julius!" I shouted, feeling like we were old friends.

"Okay. Okay." He thumped his hand against the steering wheel. "I'm thinking… thinking…"

"Well, think faster. We don't have all day."

"Bossy, bossy… you look too sweet to be so bossy."

"Yeah, yeah. Come on … spit it out. I shared, now it's your turn." But in my head, I was saying, oh my gosh, he thinks I'm sweet! I was totally crushing on him. Too bad he was taken. And the target of my client. So yeah… definitely no romance there. Not that I was looking for romance. Romance was overrated. I didn't need romance. I was fine. Just fine. Then why couldn't I stop looking at his lips?

He smiled, and I blushed. God, he totally caught me staring.

"I just want to say that you're very cute when you blush."

"I didn't blush. This car is just hot."

"So you're saying, you're just flushed?"

"You know what? Let's just get out of the car." I needed some space. It wasn't the car that was hot.

"Don't you want me to answer the question?" he asked, stepping out of the car and following me to the door of the floral shop.

"Nope. I don't care anymore."

"Yes you do."

"No I don't"

"Aww man, and I really wanted to tell you…"

I rolled my eyes and pushed the door open, but I wasn't annoyed. I needed space. And I needed to not be alone with him. My thoughts weren't exactly pure. I had to keep reminding myself that he was taken. Charming, handsome, funny, helpful, but very, very taken.

"Good morning, Julius and Ana, correct?" said the shopkeeper happily. She had big eyes that seemed even bigger behind the glasses she wore.

"Partially right," he said as he extended his hand. "I'm Julius, and this is my friend Becca. She's also our photographer. She's subbing for Ana today."

"Friend and photographer. Double duty," the shopkeeper said with a laugh. I smiled politely.

"Let's get started." She came from around the desk and shook my hand. "Nice to meet you. We have the best selection in town, come on back."

She whisked us to the back room where floral arrangements of all colors and sizes greeted us. I was instantly overwhelmed and turned to look at Julius. His eyes were comically large as he took in the scene in front of us.

"Umm… we'll just take them all," he mumbled.

The florist laughed, grabbing her sides. "You're a funny one. Let me go ahead and put the 'out for lunch' sign on the door. I'm sure this will take an hour or two."

Julius and I looked at each other in horror.

The florist didn't notice as she happily hummed a tune and disappeared into the front of the store.

"Two hours?!" I hissed. "Are you kidding me? Looking at flowers? Who spends two hours looking at flowers?"

He shrugged. "I'm just as surprised as you are." He narrowed his eyes. "Hey, you've been married before, you should know all this."

I shook my head. "I eloped."

"Smart girl."

I was really tempted to demand his car keys and tell him that I would be back in an hour, but it had taken thirty minutes just to get here.

"Maybe there's a Starbucks in the area…"

"Don't you even think about it."

"Okay, are we ready?" the florist said, reappearing.

Julius looked at me then tossed an arm around my shoulder and squeezed me tight. "Ready. So excited. You have no idea."

The huge fake smile on his face made me want to laugh, but I bit my lip, not wanting to be rude.

"Ready," I managed to say.

"Great!" the shopkeeper turned away and started talking.

I took the opportunity to knee Julius with my elbow.

"Hey," he said, letting go of me.

"I might hate you a little right now," I hissed in a whisper.

He responded by giving me a genuine smile. "This is going to be so much fun. You'll see." He slid in arm around my shoulder again, but this time I didn't pull away.

AN HOUR LATER, my nose felt clogged and my stomach was growling. I stopped listening about thirty minutes ago.

I was leaning against a wall, pretending to be looking at flower arrangement options on my phone. I was actually playing Candy Crush.

"So I think we're all done here," I heard Julius say.

Finally, thank God. I looked up from my phone.

"Find anything interesting?" he asked me, his tone serious but his eyes anything but. He was such a joker.

"Nope. I think Ms. Morales knows her stuff. I'm sure the arrangements will look spectacular."

Ms. Morales beamed and so did I. Julius shook his head and mouthed, "You should be ashamed of yourself."

I held back a laugh and told them that I would wait in the car while he wrapped things up.

Happily, I made my way to the car and waited for

Julius. I texted Dana and Piper while I was busy doing nothing.

Finally, Julius came out of the shop. He opened his mouth to tell me something when his phone rang.

He pulled it out of his pocket, ready to ignore it when he suddenly frowned and answered.

He was short with whomever was on the phone. He unlocked the car, unsmiling with the phone still against his ear.

"Fine," he said to the person on the other line as I slid in. His hands were tight on the wheel, and his whole body language had changed. Whomever was on the other line wasn't exactly his favorite person.

"Yeah," he said into the phone as he pulled off. He glanced at me and finally gave me a big smile. "Becca was a great help."

I smiled at the glint in his eyes and the underlying sarcasm in his tone. I was the opposite of helpful.

"I gotta get off the phone. I'm driving, and it's a madhouse out here."

I looked at him in surprise. There wasn't another car in sight.

"Okay, will do. I'll add that to my to-do list," he mumbled absentmindedly as he hung up without a good-bye.

"Sorry about that," he said while literally throwing his phone behind him and into the back seat.

I didn't want to seem nosey, but I couldn't help but ask, "Was that your worst enemy or something?"

"Close… Annie's mom."

"Oh?" I said, pretending to not know that she wasn't exactly his favorite person.

"Trust me, she dislikes me ten times as much as I dislike her."

"I can see that."

He settled into the seat, adjusting his shoulders as if he were tense. He had wide shoulders. Strong shoulders.

I turned away from him and said, "Mind if I turn on some music?"

"I don't mind at all. Let me guess. You're a Metallica fan?"

I didn't even know who Metallica was.

I shook my head. "I just like whatever they plan on the radio."

"Top 40?"

"You say that as if it's a bad thing."

"How about Iron Maiden?"

"Who?"

"Okay, how about Ozzy Osbourne?"

"Hey, wasn't Sharon Osbourne on America's Got Talent?"

He sighed heavily and nodded. "Yes, that's his wife."

"See… I sort of know what you're talking about."

"Okay, how about Marilyn Manson? That's sort of contemporary?"

"Ewww… he's creepy. I saw one of his music videos from back in the 90s. I think my mom used to listen to him when she was younger."

He started to laugh. "Stop it. You're making me feel old."

"Old? Aren't you like my age?"

"I'm thirty-seven."

"Oh."

"I have good genes."

"Clearly. You're like almost forty but you still look good." I immediately wanted to hide my face. Had I seriously just told him that he was attractive? "I mean, you look good for someone who's almost middle-age." That was a nice recovery.

"Middle-age?" he said, clearly offended. "Forty is like the new twenty."

"Ummm twenty is the new twenty," I couldn't help but say.

He laughed, and I smiled. I liked how easily he laughed. I liked making him laugh.

I laid my head back against the headrest and was going to close my eyes when he said, "I had a stuffed teddy bear named Walter that I carried everywhere with me until I was at least twelve."

My eyes widened, and I looked at him in confusion

and then I remembered. "So that's your secret that you don't tell anyone?" I wanted to laugh.

"Not a soul," he said with a smile.

"Walter," I said to myself as I closed my eyes again, "cute."

Julius was full of surprises.

* * *

"So how's the new job going?"

"Pretty easy," I said to Dana. "The guy I'm following around is so hot."

Dana gave me a nod of approval. "Finally, some eye candy. Maybe he could be the one."

"He's getting married, remember?"

"Oh yeah, oh well… so are you following him around today?"

"Nope. I'm meeting him and his future wife at a fancy botanical garden place. I need to take photos for their wedding invitations."

"Sounds like fun."

"I mean, I'm also supposed to find some evidence that he's a terrible person."

"That shouldn't be hard. Most people kind of suck."

"Dana…."

"Well, they do."

"Anyway, I really don't think I'll find what my client

wants me to find. He seems to be a genuine guy. Really nice."

"I don't know… you can't really trust the nice ones."

"Carter's nice."

"He's the exception."

I couldn't help but laugh. "You're too much."

"I know. Anyway, if you need any help following him, I am available."

The last time I let Dana go with me to follow one of the many cheaters, she set off a car alarm and insisted on wearing a trench coat and sunglasses. To say I was immensely embarrassed would be an understatement.

"I think I'm good. No help needed. Thanks though."

She poked out her lower lip. "You don't want my help."

I reminded her of how she "helped" me last time.

"That was a fluke!" she insisted.

I changed the subject. "How do you have nothing planned when you have three kids?" Meredith was from her marriage to Tom and the twins were from her second marriage.

"They're hanging out with Carter's parents."

"Nice."

"Having three different sets of grandparents to drop the kids off with is a godsend."

"Except…"

"Now that I have so much time on my hands, I don't

know what to do with myself. Maybe I should start working out again."

"Or not," we said at the same time.

"You know me too well."

"Well, we are kind of like sister wives."

Dana laughed, and I couldn't help but still be in awe that we had the same ex-husband but were still able to be friends. It was rough to start. She hated me, but she came around when she realized how dedicated I was to Meredith. I was pretty young at the time and kind of not the best role model, since I wanted to take her to Vegas and all that, but I matured and grew over the years and luckily so had my relationships. At least, all the ones that truly mattered.

After I said bye to Dana I made my way over to the botanical garden where I was told to meet Julius, Ana, and the rest of the wedding party. I knew Claire was probably unhappy with me because I hadn't found any dirt on Julius yet. I needed to get some surveillance done. After all, I didn't expect Julius to do something at one of his pre-wedding events that would be question-able. What did Claire expect him to do? Get drunk during a toast and confess that he was guilty of embezzlement? Or maybe she expected him to smack one of the bridesmaids on the butt?

I couldn't imagine any of those things happening. Julius seemed like a stand-up guy. I didn't know why she didn't trust him. And I was pretty convinced she just didn't want someone like Julius to be with her daughter. She was the type who would have approved of someone like my ex-husband. Uptight, wealthy, controlling, traditionally employed, but lacking character. Yep, that was the type of person that I was sure would get Claire's stamp of approval.

I had a job to do, but this was the first time I felt that I wouldn't find anything. I shrugged to myself. I would just take some pretty pictures until either Claire gave up or Julius decided to go against his nature and do something wrong. I couldn't see that happening. Ana was lucky. I didn't believe in fairy tales. After all, I was married and divorced just barely out of my teens, but I did believe that what Anna and Julius had was special.

I got to the venue only to find everyone gathered outside of it. "Hey, what's going on?" I asked one of the groundskeepers. I hoped he or she was a groundskeeper. They had on a uniform with the name of the park on it.

"Someone reported a gas leak in the area."

"You can't be too careful with those pipelines," Claire said, coming to stand next to me. "I guess you have the day off," she said meaningfully and walked away.

I didn't know what she was hinting at. Was she the one who called about a gas leak? If so, she was pretty ruthless. Wow. She didn't even want invitations going out? The lady was determined, that was for sure.

But it would be a good day to follow him around. Speaking of him, he and Ana were walking in my direction. He was dressed so nicely in a suit that did nothing to hide how strong his body was. I was surprised to find he could find a suit to fit him. He kind of reminded me of a younger Thor.

"Hey, so you probably heard from Claire there was a gas leak. We're not going to chance it. We'll just reschedule for another time and pay you for the day."

I bit my lip feeling crazy guilty. He didn't know that I was already getting paid to find dirt on him. Technically, for this job I was getting paid twice. He was paying me. Claire was paying me. I couldn't take his money. I had some morals, after all.

"It's no problem. Don't bother paying me. "

"How kind of you," I heard Claire say behind me. I sort of wanted to elbow her.

"You sure? It's no problem… you drove all the way here after all."

"She said don't pay her, so don't pay her. It's not like you're made of money suddenly. Because if you were, I wouldn't have to be paying for all this."

"You're paying for all this because you insisted on all this," Julius surprised me by saying.

"Well, excuse me for wanting the best for my daughter. The best that you clearly can't provide."

Oh wow. I wanted to disappear. The tension and anger between them was almost palpable.

"I'm sorry you feel that way," Julius said visibly trying to hold his anger in check. Ana stepped between them interrupting their argument.

Perfect timing. I didn't want to be the only thing in between two ticking bombs. And to be honest, I was more afraid of what Claire would say than Julius.

She seemed determined to make his life a living hell.

"Hi, Becca," Ana said, giving me a smile. "Sorry about all this. We'll pay you for today."

"She doesn't need to be paid for today, she didn't even do anything."

"But she came out of her way—"

"I'm fine, Ana. Really," I said nervously, feeling like another fight was going to break out.

"It's only fair, " Ana said.

"Oh, god, you bleed hearts and fairness. Fairness is a privilege. Life isn't about being fair."

"Thanks for the life lesson, Mom," Julius said deadpan, and Claire seemed ready to blow a fuse. I guessed she didn't like being called mom by the one person she hated. Or maybe she hated more than one person. She seemed to have a lot of hate to spread around. An equal opportunity hater, I thought to myself as I suppressed a bubble of inappropriate laughter. "We'll pay you for the day, Becca, Ana and I insist. Enjoy your day off."

"Thanks," I said, feeling sort of bad.

Claire looked pissed. "But I—"

"Mom, please," Ana said, looking embarrassed. "Enjoy your day off, Becca. I'll call you, Mom." Ana and Julius walked away and got into their car and drove off.

I headed to my car, and Claire called me as soon as I was about to pull off.

"Follow him. Find something on him. Anything. He's too good to be true. He's no prince charming. Just another frog. Do your job, Becca."

And just as abruptly as she called, she hung up.

I sighed. I guessed I was working today.

I hoped that Ana didn't plan on spending the day with Julius. They still lived separately so I discreetly waited until he dropped Ana off. He didn't stick around at her place.

I got my camera ready.

He drove to a little candy shop on the south side of town and just for the heck of it, I took pictures of him going inside. I needed proof that I had at least followed him. He smiled at the cashier, and I took pictures of that. It wasn't incriminating, but at least it would give Claire something to smile about at night. I kind of pictured her as Cruella De Ville. If I had to play the role of a Disney princess, then she would definitely play the role of the villain.

She was kind of horrible. When I was younger, I sort of gave everyone the benefit of the doubt. But then I married, divorced, and grew up a heck of a lot. I liked to think I wasn't as gullible or silly as before. Gosh, I was definitely still a little flighty, but hey, I was a work in progress. Everyone was, right?

I followed him some more and took pictures half-heartedly. This was an absolute bore.

While I stalked him, he received a phone call. He was laughing with whomever was on the phone with him. I imagined his laugh. It was the best thing about him, and that was saying a lot. He was gorgeous and nice, and he had a great laugh. A wonderful laugh.

I couldn't help but compare him to Tom. Tom rarely laughed, unless it was at someone else's expense. Tom was a killjoy and not fun at all. I hadn't really dated much since Tom. I hadn't been in a serious relationship at all, actually since my marriage ended. Not that I wanted to be in another relationship. Or did I? No, I said to myself, a relationship definitely wasn't in the cards for me. I didn't want to turn into an old cat lady though, but that seemed more appealing than being alone. Maybe I would just get a dog. No. I didn't have time for a dog. Maybe just one cat then. Hmmm…

* * *

Two hours later, I was standing in front of the local animal shelter with my father who looked bewildered.

"We're going to do what here?" He looked around as if he wished he was anywhere else but there. I had forgotten that my dad wasn't really an animal person. Nor was I. I liked animals a lot, I just didn't like having to take care of them. That sounded too hard.

"Getting a cat."

"A cat. I don't want a cat."

"Dad, we just had this conversation ten minutes ago. It'll be nice to have a pet."

"Nice for who? I'm fine without one."

"Come on, Dad. Let's go look at some fluffy animals." I pulled him toward the entrance.

"No thanks…"

"You said you wanted to come along…"

"Not to the pound…"

"Daaaaadddddd," I whined and could see that he was giving in.

"Alright, let's go see these rejects."

"Dad!"

He laughed and tossed an arm around my shoulder as we went in.

Less than fifteen minutes later, we were heading back to the car.

I couldn't take it. The smell. The sounds. The absolute sadness. "That was traumatizing. All those animals needing homes."

"I told you, but you didn't listen to me. I told you it would be depressing."

"You were right."

"I'm your dad, I'm always right," he said, climbing into the driver's seat.

"Come on, Dad. Let me drive."

"Your driving frightens me."

"Thanks, Dad."

"You're welcome."

I tossed him the keys and let him drive. It gave me time to think.

"Dad, have you ever thought about getting married again?"

His eyes got big, and he started to have a coughing fit. It was a good thing we were at a red light.

"Married? God no." He shuddered, and I laughed. "Why? Are you thinking about it?"

Now it was time for my eyes to grow wide. "What? No. Definitely not. I think I'm just going to be a bachelorette forever."

He shook his head. "You're young."

"You were too."

"Don't remind me," he said with a soft laugh. And then his voice grew serious. "That's the life I chose, but don't get me wrong; if I had met someone else, someone who made my heart go pitter patter, I might have walked down the aisle again."

"Really? You never told me that."

He shrugged. "It's not something I really thought about, but I know I would have tried again, if the opportunity had come up. But it didn't."

"Awww, Dad." I didn't know he was such a romantic. "You should get out there and start dating again."

"Nope."

"Dad, come on."

"Are you kidding me? I don't know how to use those apps. And even if I did, I wouldn't want to try. I believe in letting things occur organically, you know?" he said, turning to look at me.

I raised a brow. "Did you seriously just say organically?"

"Isn't that how the cool peeps talk now? Organic this? Natural that?"

I had to laugh. "Dad, you're hilarious. But maybe you should date again? How long has it been?"

"A decade, give or take…"

"Dad!"

"What?"

"You haven't gone on a date in nearly a decade?"

"Or more," he said with a shrug. "But who are you to judge? At least I have an excuse. I'm old. What's yours?"

He was right. What was my excuse? I sat back in my seat deep in thought.

Maybe I should join one of those dating sites. Do the whole dating thing. That sounded… terrible. And then I had an idea.

"Maybe I'll ask Carter or someone to introduce me to someone… that would be cool. Right?"

"Yep. I say go for it."

I had an idea. "I'll go for it, if you do."

He was about to say no, I could tell, and my shoulders slumped in disappointment. And then he surprised me.

"What the heck. Why not?" He tossed an arm around my shoulder.

I could barely contain my excitement. "This is going to be fun."

I ignored his response of, "Or not."

* * *

LATER THAT WEEK, I watched as my dad paced back and forth in the living room. He had on a dress shirt and a pair of slacks. He was even wearing a tie. He looked nice. So handsome. I had forgotten over the years how handsome he was. Even with the slight paunch, he was a good looking man. I convinced him to cut his hair instead of combing over the bald spot.

"Soo umm, how do I look?"

"Like a young Jason Statham," I reassured him.

He looked in a mirror, sucked his tummy in, and said. "Yeah, I think you're right."

I couldn't help but laugh.

"Look at us," he said then. "Both of us with dates. What are the chances…"

Strangely enough, Meredith convinced the school librarian, Lori, to go on a date with Dad. And Dana set up a date with me and her administrative assistant at work. I was kind of looking forward to it. I didn't expect a love match, but it would be nice to at least get out there.

If love like Ana's and Julius' existed, then maybe there would be enough to go around for me. I was done being cynical. Like Dad said, I was totes too young for that.

"Well, wish me luck," he said when a car honked from out front.

I looked confused. "Hold on, how are you getting there? Is she coming to pick you up?"

"Are you kidding me? I'm taking an Uber. I haven't had a night out in forever. So if my date turns out to be a bust, I still plan to get my drink on."

"Get your drink on? Who are you or what have you done with my father?"

He laughed, kissed my forehead, and said, "Have a good time."

"You too."

He whistled as he disappeared out the door. My dad. Going on a date. In an Uber. Life sure knew how to throw twists.

I didn't know what the evening held for me, but I was excited about it. I guessed some of Dad's optimism had rolled off on me.

* * *

UNLIKE DAD, I was totally going to drive to meet my date. What if my date was psycho? I needed to make sure I could make a clean getaway.

I threw on a pair of jeans and my favorite tee. I tossed on a jacket and headed to the car. On the way, my phone rang.

It was Dana.

"Are you on your way yet? I'm so excited. You're going to love Douglas." She was gushing. I'd never heard Dana so excited.

"I'm sure he's great," I said as I slid in the car.

"He's amazing. The best. You'll see. And so handsome. Hot. He's hot. You'll love him."

The more she said it, the more I kind of doubted it. She was definitely overcompensating for something. I shrugged it off and told her I would call her back after my date.

I heard he didn't live too far from me, and we were meeting at a trendy casual dining restaurant downtown with a huge patio. I heard there was even karaoke some weeknights. I didn't plan on getting drunk enough to try that.

It turned out there was a free valet, so I handed my keys off to the man standing in tight jeans and black shirt. I guessed uniforms weren't a thing anymore. I secretly hoped I hadn't just handed my keys to a stranger, but when he turned around I saw the restaurant's logo on the back of his shirt.

I sighed in relief. Yay. I hadn't given my car keys to a car thief.

My date said he would meet me at the entrance of the restaurant. I certainly hoped he would be there soon. Now, suddenly I was nervous. How did I look? Was my t-shirt a stupid idea? Was I dressed too casually? Oh god, maybe I should just go home.

"Becca?" said a voice behind me.

I turned around and made myself swallow. God he was hot. He was tall with long brown hair that almost touched his shoulders. He had hazel eyes and a warm, inviting, smile.

"Becca?" he said again, now looking a little unsure of himself.

I finally found my voice. "Yeah, and you must be Douglas."

He extended his hand formally, and I took it, his large palm swallowing my own. It was then that I saw the tattoos that went straight up his arm. Sexy. Definitely the opposite of Tom. I felt that I was winning already, no matter how this night turned out.

He reached for my hand and said with a small, sexy smile, "Shall we?"

"Yes, we shall," I said, letting him lead me into the restaurant.

It was loud, as I expected, and he surprised me by leaning down and saying, "Want to go out to the patio where it's not so crazy?"

I nodded, trying to ignore the little flashes of heat that I felt when his breath touched my ear. He was sexy, available, and so far polite. Nice. And he was considerate. Definitely a winner. I so wanted to text Dana a version of my happy dance.

The patio was adorned with little Christmas lights, and fake palm trees were placed strategically around the space. There was a blues band playing that night, and we sat a little far off from it so that we could actually hear each other speak. I wasn't a fan of blues, but I liked live music. The band was clearly good, and couples were already on the dance floor. The evening seemed primed for romance. There was moonlight, music, and a gentle breeze. It was almost magical. While I took in our surroundings, a waitress came out and we ordered a few drinks. It turned out that Douglas didn't drink, but he didn't mind if I did.

Wow. It seemed an extra bonus that I wouldn't have to worry about him getting sloppy drunk. Before Piper met Ty, she had plenty of stories of her dates ending up as drunken slobs in the back of a taxi.

We talked about his job and what it was like to work for Dana. I told him a little bit about what I did. I didn't tell him the sordid details, but my stories of cheating spouses did make him laugh.

"So did you ever think that you would be making a living off of following around people with questionable morals?"

"Nope. I'm pretty sure that's a career my advisor never considered for me."

We both laughed and he ran a hand through his hair. He seemed hesitant about what he was about to say next, but continued anyway. "Don't take this the wrong way, but it seems that both of us are sort of just floating through life trying to find our place."

I hadn't thought about it before, but he was right. "That's exactly how I feel."

"So tell me about your last date."

I thought hard about it, and he called me on it. "You don't even remember, do you?"

"No," I said, feeling self-conscious. I didn't want him to think I was some sort of dateless loser. "I'm so busy with work that I don't get a chance to date much."

"I get it," he said, taking a sip of his soda.

"How about you? When was your last date?"

He rubbed a hand through his hair, and his tight shirt pulled at his muscles. God, he had a great body. He was yummy to look at. So yummy that I totally forgot I had asked him a question. I needed to focus.

"It was a total disaster," was the part I heard. I grimaced, as if I knew what he was talking about.

"So what do you really want to do? If money were no object," he asked, changing the subject again.

"Sleep?"

He laughed, "Come on." He nudged my arm playfully. "Open up a little. I won't tell anyone, I promise."

"A travel photographer," I said instantly. "I would travel the world and take photos."

"So why don't you do that?"

I laughed, "I can't. I can't just…"

"Why not? What's stopping you?"

"I—I… maybe… I don't know."

What was stopping me? I wasn't married. I didn't have any children. Yeah, I was trying to help dad with a few bills, but I really didn't have an excuse for not pursuing what I wanted. So what exactly was my problem? "How about you, what would you like to do?"

"Animation," he said without hesitation.

"Like video games?"

He smiled "Actually no. Like cartoons. Love your shirt by the way."

I was wearing a shirt with my favorite cartoon character.

"So what's stopping you from making cartoons?"

He laughed, "Well, besides the fact that I know nothing about animation and can't draw."

We laughed together and then he tilted his drink toward mine. "Here's to our dreams," he said as he clinked his glass against mine. "And making them happen… someday."

"Here's to that."

"You're lucky, though," he said, catching me off guard, "At least you're sort of doing something related to what you love."

"I really don't think taking pictures of cheaters counts."

"Hey, you have to start somewhere," he joked, and then he leaned in and said, "Want to dance?"

I wanted to say no, but I was here with a sexy man feeling kind of carefree for once in my lifetime. I felt that maybe dreams could come true. Why not?

So against my better judgement, I said yes.

He pulled me into his arms and twirled me around the patio. I didn't care who was around as I clumsily tried to keep up. I just enjoyed dancing, and having fun was a welcomed change. I had forgotten how good it felt.

And just as I was finally relaxing and hoping maybe this evening would lead to something more, I heard someone say "Dougie?"

Immediately, Douglas let me go. Unfortunately, I was in full spin when he did, and I ended up tripping over my own feet and falling unceremoniously into the lap of the guitar player.

A guitar player who I knew.

"Hey, Becca," said Julius, holding on to me as I balanced precariously on his lap.

I tried to right myself, and he helped me as best as he could. I was so embarrassed. I felt like I spent every moment of my life embarrassed or humiliated in some form or fashion. I said as much to him as he helped me up. The other band members were staring and me, and I just wanted to run off and hide. What the heck just happened? One moment I was dancing with a beautiful man, and the next I was in Julius' lap. Not that Julius' lap was a bad place to be, I couldn't help but think to myself, but how I arrived there wasn't my most graceful moment, that was for sure.

"Where is... What?" I didn't know what to say. I didn't know what was going on, and my back was kind of sore since I practically impaled myself on the guitar when I landed on Julius.

"I think that right there might answer all your questions."

I looked to where he was pointing and saw Douglas talking to a full-figured woman who seemed to be in tears. He was comforting her, and then he brought her into his arms. That moment was so tender, so heart-felt as he held her gently, that it was clear, without a doubt that they were together. They were a couple. The way he held her as if she was the most delicate thing in the world and the way she circled her arms around his neck as if she never wanted to let go, made me want to cry.

"Sorry about your date," he said, and I shrugged. I didn't know what to say. A moment ago I was dancing around with a dream guy and then I literally came crashing back to earth.

"Sorry. I've got to get out of here."

I pulled away from him and gathered my purse quickly. I dashed outside and waited anxiously for my car.

I heard Douglas calling out to me, and I was ready to lash out at him, but the look on his face was so apologetic.

"You didn't tell me that you invited your girlfriend."

He looked so guilty. "That's Tera. My ex-girlfriend… We broke up recently. It's complicated. We're high school sweethearts. I mean, we were... and now... anyway. I'm sorry. I didn't know she would be here. It was a shock. I'm sorry... I ... uh... I gotta go. I'm so sorry, but I wish you all the best."

I knew he wasn't a jerk. I just felt like he was. I sighed and said, "I get it. Go be with her."

He hugged me abruptly, practically squeezing the life out of me. "Thanks for understanding."

And then he was gone, and once again I was alone.

"Where's the stupid valet with my car?" I said to myself. I was beyond embarrassed and just wanted to disappear. And yell at Dana. I wanted to yell at her for setting me up with someone who was still stuck on his ex. And whose ex was still stuck on him.

I pulled out my phone to call her when someone called out my name.

"What is it?" I snapped, turning toward Julius.

"Sorry."

"No, I... it's been a tough night."

"Hey, you want to get out of here?"

"I'm trying..." I groaned.

"Leave your car. I know a place just down the street. Empty and no one around who probably witnessed your humiliation."

"Thanks, Julius, but no thanks."

"Come on... Just a few minutes. It'll take your mind off of things."

I could go home and lick my wounds, or I could spend some time in good company. I didn't feel like being alone tonight, so I took Julius up on his offer.

We walked in silence down the block. I was grateful for the silence. And I was second guessing myself. I should have just gone home. God, I couldn't do anything right. I couldn't even date right. I really hoped Dad was having better luck than me. I was a disaster. My life was a disaster.

"Stop it," he said, catching me off guard.

"Stop what?"

"Beating yourself up."

"I can't. I'm embarrassed. Like super humiliated. Listen, I think I'm just going to go home."

"One drink. And then you can go home and mope, and I won't stop you."

I stared at him and he stared back at me, neither of us speaking. Apparently, we were in some sort of staring contest.

"Fine," I said giving in.

"Great, you won't regret this." He opened the door to a tavern I hadn't noticed before.

Inside it was warm and fairly quiet, but the smell of the place... Oh my, it smelled like all kinds of deliciousness. "What is this?" I said looking around. It didn't look like a bar or smell like one. "I thought you said we were getting a drink."

"Well, I'm starving, but you looked like you could use a drink."

He was right, I could use a drink, but now I was hungry. The smell of sautéed garlic and onions made my stomach growl. "Is this some sort of Asian noodle bar?"

"Sure is. And it's BYOB."

"Did you bring anything?"

"Nope. I don't carry beer in my pocket."

He had a point. I just needed to stop talking.

I sat at the nearest table and tried to ignore the sudden strong hunger pains. Douglas and I hadn't made it to dinner. I morosely wondered if he was having dinner with Tera right now. They were probably gazing into each other's eyes and holding hands.

"You look angry."

"I am," I said honestly.

"You should be. I make it a point to not throw my date across the dance floor."

I couldn't help but smile. "That's very chivalrous of you."

"I try to be."

"Soooo, did he tell you who the special lady was?"

"His ex. They just broke up."

"Like when? Yesterday?"

I shrugged. "Can we change the subject?" I didn't want to keep discussing my disaster of a date. "I didn't know you were in a band. And a blues band for that matter."

"Hold that thought," he said. "I'm going to order us some food. What would you like? Pho for you or something else?" he said, referring to a Vietnamese soup.

"I'll take whatever. I'm not picky."

"That would explain your date."

"Ha ha," I said humorlessly, but I appreciated his attempt at humor. If I couldn't laugh at myself, then what was the point of even having a sense of humor?

He went up to the counter and ordered for us. I stared at him while he ordered.

He was a nice guy. He should have been performing with his band, but he was here with me. And he didn't have to be. He was just naturally a caring individual, always coming to Ana's rescue, and now he was coming to mine. Ana was a lucky girl.

He turned around then and smiled at me. Such a nice guy, I thought again to myself as I smiled back.

"Soup, madame," he said, placing a bowl of steaming noodles and broth covered with herbs in front of me. He ordered the same for himself and sat across from me.

I leaned forward over my bowl and inhaled deeply. "Hmm, that smells delicious."

We ate in silence. He didn't ask me about my date. We didn't talk at all. After I was done, I pushed my bowl away and sighed.

"This is nice."

"It is. Sometimes silence really is golden."

"Wow, you sound old."

He tossed a napkin at me, and I dodged it.

"So how did you meet Ana?" I asked. When I asked Ana earlier, I hadn't gotten very much information, so I figured why not ask Julius directly. Claire was right about one thing, Ana wasn't much of a sharer. Getting information from her was sort of like pulling teeth.

"We had a mutual friend."

"Oh? Is your friend coming to the wedding? I haven't met him or her yet, right?" So far, I don't think I had met anyone from the wedding party.

He looked away and taped his fingers on the table. "Him. Sam Higgins. We were all friends."

I noticed then that he was using past tense. "You guys aren't friends anymore?"

"Well, Sam passed away last year."

"Oh my God, I'm so sorry."

"Yeah, Ana took it hard. They were roommates." Now things were making sense. The sneakers, the jerseys, the motorcycle helmet. I noticed all those things in her apartment and assumed they belonged to Julius.

"How did he die, if you don't mind me asking?"

"Motorcycle accident. A reckless driver didn't even see him, practically plowed right over him. He died instantly."

I closed my eyes, unable to stomach how terrible that must have been.

"I'm so sorry."

"Me too. Sam was a great guy. He used to play sax. That's actually how we met. He was part of the band. And Ana quit the band after Sam died."

"Ana was part of it?"

"More than part of it. She was the heart of it. She did all the lead vocals."

I was surprised. Ana was part of a band and could sing? Wow. Now it all made sense. Didn't her mother say that Ana at one point wanted to major in music?

"And so that's how you and Ana became close…"

"Yeah," he said gruffly, reaching for an empty straw wrapper. I knew he needed something to do with his hands to distract himself from the painful memories. I was the same. I only fidgeted when I was feeling emotional.

I found myself reaching for his hand and squeezing it. "I'm sorry you lost your friend."

He met my eyes, and under his gaze I realized that the last thing I wanted to do was look away or let go. And I knew at that moment, he felt it too. Because he was the first to pull away.

He cleared his throat. "I need to get back to the band. I'm sure they don't want to do all their sets without me."

"Oh yeah," I said, feeling bad. After all, he dropped everything he was doing to help me.

"Hopefully your guitar is still in working order," I said in an attempt to lighten the mood.

He smiled. "We'll see."

We walked in silence down the narrow sidewalks leading to the restaurant, and every now and then my hip would brush against his. I was more than aware of his nearness. I was aware of every breath he took. I was aware of the way he smelled. I was too aware of him. I was sure I was falling for him.

I sped up, wanting to get away from him. I needed to put some distance between us. I couldn't be alone with him. Not after that revelation.

"Hey, slow down. I need to get back, but I don't think we need to sprint there."

"Sorry," I said sheepishly. The valet saw me approaching and this time, he quickly went to get my car.

"I guess I'll see you next week."

"Next week?" I asked, looking at him quizzically.

"Yeah, remember? For the wedding invitations redo."

"Oh yeah. I'll be there."

The valet pulled up, and Julius held the car door while I climbed in. He was such a gentleman.

"Thanks for a great evening."

I blanked rapidly. "I should be telling you that."

He shrugged. "You landed in my lap. The rest was easy."

It felt like a date. Too much like one. I had to get out of there.

"Thanks for everything, Julius. Really."

"Anytime," he said. He reached out then and tucked a strand of hair behind my ear.

The slight gesture, the feel of his hand on my hair, sent shivers down my spine. All thoughts of my previous date went out the window, and all I could think of was what it would feel like to be held by him, comforted by him. And how lucky Ana was to have a man like him by her side.

"Be safe, Becca," he said as he pushed the car door closed, and then he disappeared into the venue.

I drove away feeling torn. I didn't want to follow him around. I didn't want to violate his privacy, and I definitely didn't want to work for Claire to make him look like a bad guy.

He clearly wasn't. I sighed. Why did life have to be so complicated?

5

"**D**id you see your itinerary?" Claire asked impatiently over the phone the next day. "I just emailed it to you."

I didn't understand. "My itinerary?" Was I going somewhere?

"Yes, we're going to check out some wedding venues out of state."

"We?"

"Well, certainly not you. Just Ana and I, so now's your chance to follow Julius."

Oh man.

"So my itinerary is what exactly?"

She sighed as if having to explain herself to a simpleton was mentally draining. "Your itinerary is a list of places that man likes to hang out." She said man as if it was a bad word.

"It was so hard to convince Ana to go with me without him," she whined.

Well, he is her fiancé, I wanted to say, but controlled myself.

"So I'm just supposed to stalk him while you guys are gone?" I said, giving the itinerary a glance on my phone.

"Exactly."

All his typical hangouts were local places, some I'd yet to discover. This would be fun. I frowned, I needed to get out more. My definition of fun was starting to scare me. Playing poker with my dad and following around a guy who I was falling for, but who was also off limits… Yeah, I needed to find other hobbies.

"I'm on it. If he's doing anything even slightly salacious, I'll find out."

"Wonderful." I could hear the smile in her voice. I was glad that something made her smile. She wasn't a complete ice queen. Just almost a complete ice queen.

I finished up the conversation with her and sat in front of my computer and stared at the itinerary. I laughed when I came across a familiar place on the list. It was the same venue I had gone to last night. I definitely wasn't going to spy on him there. I was sure that after last night's fiasco I was a bit too memorable to chance that. I wondered if he would be there though. I felt like a love-struck teenager hoping she'd run into her crush. Snap out of it, I told myself, you have a job to do.

I knew I wouldn't find anything, but I still needed to make it appear as if I was trying. It was time for a stake-out. I planted myself in a cheap rental car across the street from his home and put on a wig. The wig was also cheap and looked it, but I didn't plan to get close enough for Julius to question the quality.

I placed my hands behind my head and hoped he didn't have neighborhood cops who might swing by and catch me. I wasn't a very good liar, and I was sure admitting to stalking someone wouldn't be something the cops would like to hear.

At eight o'clock sharp Julius left his house, and I followed him wishing I was a real detective and had a way to tap his phone or set up a camera at his house. There were things I would rather do like sleep in late than follow Julius around for absolutely no reason.

Alas, I wasn't a real detective and needed the money, so I just did what I was told. I really wondered what Claire expected me to find. What kind of wrongdoing did she think Julius was capable of? Was she hoping that I would get a pic of him flirting with a waitress or, even better yet, meeting up with a secret lover? I laughed at the absurdity of it all.

We pulled up to a bakery, and I frowned. I sincerely doubted that his secret lover would be there. But who knew? Maybe he was having an affair with the sugar cookies? I would totally have an affair with sugar cookies. I would just sit around and eat them all day.

I made myself focus on the task in front of me instead of fantasizing about sugar cookies. I watched as Julius walked in and I reached for my camera. From what I could tell, he bought what seemed to be a box of muffins or maybe cookies, tipped the cashier, and then walked away. So far, he seemed to be an upstanding guy, but we were only on his first stop. Who knew what conniving, no-good things he planned to do with those muffins, I thought to myself with a giggle.

The next stop was a gated retirement village. I couldn't go in there. But it seemed Julius wasn't either. Instead, he got out of his car and started chatting with the security guard. He handed him the box, said a few words, gave him a hug and then left.

I wondered what that was all about.

Finally, he made his way to the coffee house where we had originally met. He wasn't scheduled to be there until sometime in the afternoon, but I guessed he needed his coffee earlier. I knew I couldn't get close enough without him noticing me so I stayed in the car.

I sat there playing on my phone not expecting much action. An hour passed, and then two. I was terrible at stakeouts. I needed to stretch my legs.

I pulled into the parking lot of a little park behind the

coffee house where a bunch of nannies or stay-at-home moms were hanging out with their kiddos. A few gave me curious looks as I walked around, clearly kid-less. I ignored the looks and stretched while letting out a big yawn. And, of course, my stomach growled. I missed breakfast.

"Fancy meeting you here," said a voice.

I instantly tensed, but downplayed my surprise. "Hi, Leona."

"What's up with the wig? It looks terrible."

I shrugged. "Just trying out a new look."

"It's not working for you," she said, lighting her cigarette. "I'm supposed to be meeting a client here. Not that you need to know that. Speaking of which, you ready for another assignment?"

I wasn't the type to say no to money offered, and she hadn't offered me an assignment for a while now. "Of course, sure." I would just figure out a way to work it around Julius' schedule.

"It should be pretty easy. Another girlfriend or wife, whatever, who thinks her significant other is probably cheating. It might mean you have to visit a titty bar."

Great, I thought sarcastically, so the lighting will be terrible. It was a sad day that my main concern about strip clubs was their terrible lighting and not what actually went on in them.

"I'll text you the details. Maybe you can use the

money to buy a better wig." She let out a hackle that soon turned into a terrible cough.

"You need to stop smoking." I couldn't help myself. She sounded as if she was about to cough up a lung.

"Who are you? My doctor? Just have your phone on, Ms. Surgeon General. I don't pay you for your medical advice; I pay you to take pictures."

She took a long drag of her cigarette, and I bid her goodbye. She didn't bother to reply. Which was fine and expected.

I made my way to my car and scanned the parking lot to make sure Julius' car was still where it was supposed to be.

It was.

I looked at my watch and sighed. I was bored. I placed my head on the steering wheel and tried not to yawn for the hundredth time.

I brought my head up just in time to watch Julius walk out of the coffee house with a short blonde. She had her arm laced around his, and I was in shock for a moment. This was too easy and completely unexpected, I thought as I picked up my camera and began to snap pictures.

She leaned toward him and seemed to be about to plant a kiss on his lips when he stepped back and straight off the porch of the small cafe. He landed in a flower bed, and I tried not to laugh.

He floundered around, and the woman moved to help him. He batted her hands away, and I couldn't help but laugh now. Whoever she was, he sure didn't want her there. He dodged her kiss and clearly didn't want her help.

Finally, he extracted himself from the bushes, and she began to dust him off. Conspicuously letting her hand go where no hand should be going in public.

Even from the distance, I could see Julius was growing angry. He tossed his hands up and said something to her. He looked pissed. He then turned away and stomped to his car. She followed behind him grabbing at his arm. I couldn't hear what was being said, but I snapped picture after picture. It was clearly a heated exchange. Finally, he climbed into his car. He looked so angry and drove away without another glance at the woman.

The woman placed her hands on her hips and watched him drive away, then climbed into her car and went in the opposite direction. I snapped a few photos of her license plate. I was hoping the photos would help me figure out who she was. Frankly, I had no idea how I would find out that kind of information, but it couldn't be that hard, right?

Since Julius was leaving off schedule, I had no idea where he was going. I circled around a few times wondering.

Things were off to a great start, I thought sarcastically when I couldn't find him. I drove a couple miles in the direction he went. I didn't see any signs of his car.

I knew where his next stop was going to be, so I went there instead. It was a Cross Fit gym in an old warehouse in the east part of town where empty warehouses were turned into luxury apartments and storefronts. I tried to think of what people called Cross Fit gyms. They didn't call them gyms, right? I thought they were called a box? I was getting Cross Fit confused with boxing. I couldn't remember what fancy name Cross Fitters used. I just knew that I had at least solved one mystery. I now knew how Julius stayed so sexy.

I waited patiently for Julius, hoping he would show up to the gym with no shirt on. He arrived about thirty minutes before he was supposed to be there. He climbed out of the car with a duffel bag and disappeared into the warehouse. He was definitely wearing a shirt, and there was no sign of the blonde this time. I sort of had a feeling that Claire might have paid the blonde to put on that little performance. It was too convenient for my taste.

As I waited for something juicy to happen, I flipped through the pictures. In every picture, you could clearly see the confusion on Julius' face. And then contempt as he pulled himself out of the bushes, and she helped brush him off. I giggled a little. It was pretty funny.

The rest of the day was uneventful. Nothing raunchy happened, and by the time four pm rolled around I was bored out of my mind. All Julius did was work, workout, work some more and then he headed home. If anything, his life was more boring than mine was.

The next day was pretty much the same and the day after next. The blonde never returned, so I was still curious about that. I sent pictures to Claire and took on Leona's assignment while I waited for Claire to get back to me. I didn't know what she planned to do with the pictures. They didn't make Julius look guilty. They made him look like he was being assaulted by a crazy lady.

That weekend, I prepped for the debauchery of the strip club. I knew it would be weird to show up on my own, so I asked Dana and Piper to come with me. To my surprise, they happily agreed.

"I've never been in one before," Piper said excitedly.

"Me neither," Dana said.

"What do we even wear?" Piper asked.

"And does it smell like cheap perfume and sex?"

That question came from Dana, of course. I wrinkled my nose. "Not that I remember, but I've never been to a strip club for guys. I've only been to the all-male revue in Vegas."

"How was that?"

"Um ... highly uncomfortable. Just male parts on display. Lots of screaming, desperate women. Kind of gross, oily men. And sweaty backs. Lots of sweaty backs."

Dana nodded. "Yep that sounds about right."

Despite my less than stellar review of strip clubs, that evening, we all piled into my car and headed to the strip club. The bouncer gave us a huge smile as we approached.

"How much is it?" I asked, reaching into my purse.

"Aww, you're customers?" he said with a wry smile. "I was hoping you ladies were here for an interview."

Dana guffawed, "Trust me. No one wants to see my mom bod. Unless you want people to pay me to keep my clothes on."

I couldn't help but laugh at her comment and so did the bouncer who let us all in for free.

"Drinks are on me," he said, winking at Dana. "And for the record," he gave Dana a wide grin, "I would pay good money to see you with your clothes off."

Dana blushed and rushed inside. "What a gross but somehow flattering comment," she said while the rest of us laughed.

The strip club was dark inside. There were tables and booths lining the walls and sprinkled here and there throughout the venue. A bar that led to a stage was the primary focus, and all the tables and booths were situated in the direction of the stage.

A few topless waitresses were making their rounds.

Dana sighed wistfully to herself after our waitress took our orders. We "I remember when my boobs were perky. Three kids and years of breastfeeding later, not so much."

Piper chimed in, "At least you have kids to blame. I was born with saggy boob-itis."

I smothered a giggle. Dana and Piper were hilarious.

The place was packed with men, but there were a few couples here and there. There was also a man sitting alone at a table with what seemed to be an emotional support dog. I just shrugged. To each their own. I did wonder what the bouncer had to say about that, though.

I wasn't a germaphobe, but I was sort of scared to touch the tables. I just didn't know how often they were cleaned or what was on them. I could only imagine. Gross. I felt strip clubs were for degenerates.

The lights were dimmed even lower, and a woman came out on stage. She had a huge boa around her neck, and she started doing these weird hip dips as she made her way downstage. The crowd started whistling and clapping enthusiastically. I didn't know what all the hoopla was about. And to be honest, even the dancer seemed bored as she walked from dude to dude gyrating and they stuck money in the waistband of her panties.

I scanned the crowd, not seeing the guy I was supposed to be spying on yet, when a group of raucous young men came in. And just like that, I found my assignment. He was leading the crew. He was already clearly drunk, and he marched right up to the front and started doing a little dance of his own. He then climbed on a bar stool and started wiggling and jiggling.

He was apparently wiggling and jiggling a bit too much because he suddenly lost his balance and fell face forward, hitting his chin on the bar. He hit the floor with a loud thud. At least, I imagined it was a loud thud. The music was too loud to actually hear it. His friends rushed over to help him up, and even the stripper stopped dancing.

She looked down at them with disgust before marching away, not bothering to finish her set. I didn't blame her. What a jerk.

I remembered then that I was supposed to be getting pictures. It was too bad I hadn't caught his little dance on camera. It was unfortunate that he was knocked out on the floor; that didn't make for good photos.

I took some pictures anyway, only half caring. Maybe Leona could use them, maybe she wouldn't. We would see.

As I placed my camera back in my purse, I noticed one of the friends looking at me curiously. My mouth opened and then closed. Goddammit. It was Julius. He continued to stare at me until he passed by, helping the others drag their friend out.

"Why was that guy eyeing you?" Dana asked.

"Yeah, that was so weird. Stalker alert. Yikes. But he was cute, so maybe he could be a winner," Piper chimed in.

I shook my head as if trying to clear it. "He's the guy that I've been following around."

"Hold on, your client's enemy? The one who's getting married?"

"Yep."

"Uh oh. You think he recognized you?"

"Or saw you taking pictures? You weren't exactly subtle," Dana added for good measure. That was so Dana.

I sighed and buried my head in my palms. "Oh nooooo ... what am I going to do?"

My phone beeped with an incoming text. I immediately reached for my phone and gulped hard when I saw that the text was from Julius.

"I'm outside. Can we talk?"

My hands shook as I sat the phone on the table. "You guys, he wants me to meet him outside."

"Who?"

"Julius."

"Who's Julius?"

"The guy. The one who just saw me taking pictures. At least, I think he saw me. Why else would he want me to meet him outside?" Both Piper and Dana were looking at me in confusion.

"How do you know he knows it's you?" Piper asked, looking confused.

"Umm, because he just texted me."

"Oh."

"Don't go. Just pretend that you don't know what he's talking about."

"That's terrible advice," Dana said.

"Try it. It might work," Piper reassured me.

I figured there was nothing to lose. "What should I say?"

"Don't listen to Piper. Please don't. That's a terrible plan. You can't just pretend to not know that he noticed you."

"Don't listen to Dana. I'm the queen of bad plans, but this is a good one. Trust me." I didn't trust Piper. Before she met Ty, she had literally dated clowns. She didn't show the best judgement.

"Okay, so tell him that you're home in bed," Piper suggested.

"Don't tell him that."

"Do you have a better idea?" Piper demanded.

"Just go out there and see what he wants. There's a possibility he never saw the camera."

"Dana's right. Maybe he didn't see the camera." I felt if I said it aloud, I could make it true.

Piper shrugged, her feelings clearly hurt because her plan was vetoed.

"I'll be right back. It'll be fine, I'm sure."

They nodded in encouragement, but I knew as soon as I turned my back they would exchange knowing looks with each other.

I slid off the stool and made my way outside. He was standing with his back against his car.

As I approached him, I tried to get my story together. I would tell him that I was just taking a pic of his friend because I thought it was funny. Yeah. That sounded plausible. Totally plausible.

He looked handsome leaning against the car. He had on dark gray dress pants, a black and white dress shirt with a collar that peeked over the gray sweater he wore on top of it. He was dressed more like a guy going to a casual meeting than a guy going to a strip club. I wondered how Ana felt about him going to a strip club. Maybe I could use that question as leverage.

He didn't smile as I approached. Instead, he crossed his arms over his chest and watched me without expression. I couldn't read his face. I couldn't read his eyes. For once, he wasn't an open book. I couldn't read his emotions. Uh oh. This wasn't going to be good.

I gave him a watery smile which he didn't return.

"Hi," I said, suddenly forgetting my plan and what I was going to say to him.

"Hi, now tell me why you're following me."

6

I wanted to jump in my car and pretend this night never happened. Darn it. I shouldn't have been so greedy and taken this stupid assignment. I should have just told Leona that I was too busy. And now I had to face the consequences.

"I'm not following you," I blurted out. Yes, lying. That was a good place to start. Now I just needed to be convincing.

He tilted a brow. "Oh really? So you just happened to be parked across the street at the coffee house several days in a row, and you just so happened to be here tonight?"

Wow. I wasn't as stealth as I thought.

"I uhhh… I wasn't following you. I was trying to follow your friend. I thought maybe he would be hanging out with you." I felt proud of myself for coming up with such a convincing lie so quickly.

"And why exactly were you following him then?"

Half-truth time. "I do some freelance work for a local P.I sometimes. And I was hired to follow your friend around."

"Hired by who?"

I shrugged and lied, "I don't know. My employer didn't share too much info. You know... privacy reasons."

He considered that for a moment, and when he finally spoke it wasn't what I wanted to hear. "I don't believe you. Try again. Did Claire hire you?"

"Nooooo," I said, probably a bit too forcefully. "Why would you think that? That's ridiculous. I don't... I mean... I barely know her."

He continued to study me. "I have all night," he said. "So spill it. Tell me who you are and why you're following me."

"I'm Becca... as you already know..." I was stalling and didn't know what I was talking about. I just figured if I talked enough I could get myself out of this mess.

"So that's really your name? You didn't lie about that; you're just lying about everything else."

"No."

"Try again."

His voice was cold. And I felt like crying. I hated

confrontation. And I hated that it looked like he didn't trust me. Well, he didn't trust me. He didn't even know me.

"So, let me guess: Claire paid you to follow me? And she probably arranged for that little blonde to throw herself at me."

I didn't say a word. I didn't know what to say.

"It's okay, you don't have to confirm it. It's clear. So did she think she would catch me cheating or something? And how long have you been following me?"

"Not long." I felt so stupid. This was my chance to explain myself, yet I couldn't say much at all.

"It's not what you think," I said, trying again.

"Then explain. Go ahead. I'm a patient man."

"She was just worried about Ana, and I really needed the money."

He was silent for a long moment and then said, "How much is she paying you? I would like to know exactly how much my privacy being violated is worth."

I winced. I felt terrible.

"She wanted some dirt on you. She wanted to know if you were really the guy you pretend to be."

"Pretend to be?" he laughed humorlessly.

"That sounded terrible. That came out all wrong." I realized now that I was crying. "Look," I said, "I know you're a decent guy."

"You don't know anything about me. Tell your

employer that she's been found out. Have a nice life, Becca. Whoever you are."

I didn't know what to say. He got into the car without another word, and I just stood there and watched him drive away. I didn't try to stop him. I just let him go and wiped at the tears running down my face.

My friends were suddenly standing there next to me. "So umm, I'm guessing that didn't go too well," Piper said.

"Yep. You guessed right." My voice sounded small and shaky. "You guys," I said swallowing back tears and being embarrassed about it, "I think I'll head out now. Thanks for coming along."

"Hey, are you alright?" Dana asked, grabbing my arm. "I'll be fine."

At least, I hoped I would be. I walked away from my friends and back to my car. I was glad they didn't insist on following me. I wanted to be alone.

I got in, pulled out, and turned on the music really loud to block out my thoughts. I drove home, but I couldn't make myself go in. I had to stop Julius from telling Claire that he knew. I had to stop him. I needed that money desperately. Maybe he would listen to reason. I had betrayed his trust, but I had a good reason. Right?

Without stopping to think, I texted him.

"Let me explain."

He texted me back. "I'm blocking your number."

I sighed. At least he was polite enough to tell me.

Desperate times called for desperate measures. I pulled out from the condo parking lot and headed in the direction of the one place I had no business going: his home.

Thanks to being a paid stalker, I knew exactly where to find him. I only prayed that it wasn't too late. I hoped that he hadn't confronted Claire yet.

I didn't even hesitate as I climbed out the car and marched to his front door. I knocked hard. And then I noticed the doorbell. I pushed that instead and waited for what felt like a million years.

Finally, the door opened.

"What the hell are you doing here?

I opened my mouth and then closed it. What was I doing there? This was a really bad idea. I turned and walked away, turning bright red and feeling like an idiot.

I made it all the way to my car and then saw my reflection. I looked defeated. Like a quitter. I didn't like what I saw.

Squashing how stupid I felt, I turned around and walked back to Julius' closed door and pounded on it.

While pounding, Julius ripped his door open.

"Look, you crazy person, go home before I call the police."

"Call them."

He folded his arms across his chest, looking amused and bemused at the same time. "Dragon Lady must be paying you a small fortune."

"Listen, I'm sorry. Okay. I know that's not enough. But I needed the money. Really needed it. So don't be mad at me. I was just doing my job."

"Apology not accepted. Have a nice life, Becca," he said, moving away from the doorframe and slamming the door.

I guessed I wasn't so convincing as the door slammed in my face.

But I wasn't going to give up.

I began to pound on it. "Come on, let me in," I muttered to myself.

He answered the door again. "Wow, you're persistent."

"Yeah, I am…" I tried to give him my saddest look. "Come on, just hear me out."

He looked like he wanted to do anything but that, but his face softened. I won… at least this battle.

"You have two minutes."

He walked away leaving his door open, and I followed him inside glad that he would give me a chance to explain. Not that I had anything to explain. I lied to him, followed him, and betrayed his trust all for a few thousand dollars. Well, ten thousand dollars, but that was beside the point.

The real matter was that I felt bad about it. More than anything, I didn't want Julius to see me as a bad person. I hated when anyone thought bad things about me.

I tried not to think of what to say next and instead looked around at his home. It was scarcely decorated. The only thing in it was just the bare minimum. There was a sofa, a little desk, and a dining room table. Definitely minimalist.

It was worse than my ex-husband's place. Not that, that counted; he had had an interior decorator do everything.

"Sit. Make yourself comfortable, unless you want to go through all my stuff and take notes. Feel free."

I ignored him and sat primly on the couch. At least, I tried to look prim. I probably just looked highly uncomfortable, which was fine. I felt highly uncomfortable.

"What's your problem?"

I looked at him, startled. "My problem?"

He settled on the couch across from me and tossed his feet up on the coffee table that was covered with old magazines.

"Yeah, what kind of person follows another person around and impedes on their privacy for a living? Like some sort of paparazzi or something..."

"I'm sorry. I really I am."

"Really? How sorry are you?" he asked, crossing his

arms over his chest. He still looked angry, but there was something else in his eyes. Something else that made me slightly uncomfortable.

I knew the reason I was feeling uncomfortable was because, for some reason, it sounded like he was propositioning me. That couldn't be. He was supposed to be getting married. Soon. And he was mad at me. I could still see anger there, simmering just below the surface. He managed his emotions well, but I knew he hated my guts. I suddenly lost my nerve and started mumbling.

"I don't… I should leave. I just wanted to explain…"

"Then explain."

There was an awkward pause as I pretended to not notice how attractive he was. His eyes peered into mine, and I looked away, focusing on his clothes. He had changed since I saw him at the strip club. He was wearing jeans that did little to conceal the bulge between his legs.

I wanted to go over and sit in his lap, maybe trace his lips with my tongue.

I shook my head, trying to clear my thoughts. What the hell was I thinking? I needed to keep my tongue to myself and keep my eyes off his crotch.

I stood up without preamble. "I gotta go."

"So just like that? No explanation. Nothing?"

He didn't move from his spot on the chair. He just sat there looking intimidating and gorgeous.

I lowered myself onto the couch. "I don't really have an excuse. Your future mother-in-law found out that I take pictures for a local private investigator, so she contacted me to—"

"Follow me around and find some dirt on me?" he finished.

"Exactly. So there, it totally wasn't my fault."

"It was. You didn't have to accept the job, but you did—"

"I needed the money," I said, feeling terrible to have to admit that. I didn't think I was a prideful person, but maybe I was. Or maybe I just didn't want him to feel sorry for me.

"Listen, I'm sorry. Like really sorry, and you're right… I didn't have to accept the job, but it was easy money."

He didn't say a word, so I kept talking.

"Not that, that's any excuse. I do feel bad for deceiving you. I'm sorry. I really am. For what it's worth, I know you're a decent guy. A really good guy." I shook my head, not knowing how I got myself into this mess. "You're probably the best guy I've ever met. And I mean that. I didn't give her anything incriminating. I didn't. I swear."

He still hadn't said anything as he continued to stare at me with a blank expression.

I sat back heavily against the couch and said, "Say something."

"Are you really a photographer?"

I shook my head, but then nodded. "But only as a hobby. Well, that's not technically true. I work for a P.I., so I take a lot of cases involving cheating wives/husbands."

"So I guess my case was right up your alley."

"For the record, I was at the strip club tonight to take pictures of your drunk friend, not to follow you around."

"That doesn't make me feel any better. So what? You got two for the price of one."

He was right. I was done oversharing.

"So did you find out anything interesting about me?"

His arms were still crossed, and his eyes were guarded.

"Nope. You're the most boring person I've ever followed. All I know is that you work all the time, do Cross Fit and you visit an old people's home occasionally."

"That's about right."

"Who lives at the old folks' home that you know?"

""That's none of your business."

I instantly felt contrite for asking. He was right. It definitely wasn't any of my business.

He sighed then and reluctantly said, "I might as well

tell you. I wasn't visiting anyone there. Sam's granddad works at the guard station there, so I was just dropping off some donuts to him. I probably shouldn't have, but he's the healthiest seventy-six-year old I know."

Surprised that he shared, I felt a smile form on my face. "That's really sweet of you. You really are the nicest guy I know."

He arched a brow. "You sure? Maybe I'm a bad guy with questionable motives. Isn't that what my future mother-in-law convinced you?"

"She's just my client. As soon as I met you, hung out with you, I knew she was wrong about you. But following you was just my job. It wasn't personal."

"Funny. Violating my privacy felt very personal."

He was right. To me, it was another job, but I had done something that I didn't expect him to forgive me for.

I messed up. It was partially Claire's fault, but the true fault was my own.

Why was I really at Julius' house tonight? Was I there because I was afraid he was going to tell Claire or had that just been my excuse? It wasn't Claire or the money that I was concerned about. I was trying to salvage the tenuous friendship I felt that had formed between Julius and me. I had feelings for him. I had gotten attached.

Shocked at my own thoughts, I leaned my head against the cushion of the couch and sighed deeply, I had gotten attached. And that was a no-no… not just because of my job. But because getting attached to any man was dangerous. A relationship wasn't in the cards for me. Not now and probably not ever, but what did it matter? He was engaged. I needed to keep telling myself that.

"You're quiet over there. What are you thinking about?"

I stood again. "That I shouldn't be here."

He uncrossed his arms and spread them over the back of the chair. I bit my lip, trying to not think of how inviting he appeared.

"You're right. You shouldn't be." His voice was cold. My time was up, and he was done listening to me.

I felt myself tearing up. Embarrassed, I attempted to turn away from him. But he was quicker than I was. He was suddenly standing there next to me pulling at my hand.

"Hey, are you okay?"

Something about the way he asked, the gentle tone of his voice, struck a chord and then to my utter disbelief and humiliation, I began to cry.

He didn't hesitate to pull me into his arms, and I didn't hesitate to let him. I cried against his chest, not knowing why I was so upset. It was just a job, right? He was just the job. Then why was I crying; not because I knew I would lose out on the money, but because I knew I would never see him again.

I had fallen in love, it appeared. I'd fallen for the man I had gotten to know. And it tore me apart that I wouldn't get to know him better. This was it. This was the last moment I would have with him and even that moment was stolen.

As I pondered that, I felt his hands gently stroking my back. It felt warm, reassuring, and I wanted to stay in his embrace forever.

The tears ceased and I just stayed there, motionless, feeling beneath my cheek the rhythm of his breath, enjoying being close to the steady thump of his heart. He was so warm, and I wanted nothing else but to stay like that forever. I couldn't remember the last time I had been held. Tom, my ex-husband, wasn't the affectionate type. Occasionally, he would hold my hand, unless he was trying to show off in front of someone, and then he would hug me, his trophy wife.

A tear slid from my eye again as I felt Julius reaching for my chin. I tried to tuck my chin down, but he wouldn't let me.

"Look at me," he said softly. I did as I was told, not knowing if I was ready to see what I would find there.

"This tear isn't for me, is it?" His finger trailed down my cheek, following the tearstain.

I shook my head. "No," I said, my voice sounding

husky to my own ears. "It's because I'm tired of making all the wrong decisions."

He brushed the tear away and brought his hands up to cup my cheeks. "Then make a right one," he said softly as he brought his lips to mine.

I didn't think of right and wrong as I kissed him. All I could think of was how much I wanted him. And how right it felt to let his mouth drift over mine. His lips fit mine as if they were made for me, and I moaned as I let his lips part mine.

His hands finally let go of my face and settled around my waist, pulling me against him as he deepened the kiss. I trailed my hands across his chest, wanting to feel his skin pressed against mine, suddenly frustrated by the clothing that was between us.

He placed his hands on my shoulders and slid the thin straps down my arms and began to place kisses across my exposed skin. Then his hands were pushing my shirt off my shoulders and down my hips, until my shirt hit the floor. He slowly brought his hands up and began to fondle my breasts as he kissed my neck, my collarbone, and every place in between was covered by his warm lips.

I groaned and let my head fall back, loving the feel of his warms lips against my skin, knowing that the feel of his hands on my breasts were doing things to my insides in the best of ways.

He pulled away from me and took my hand. I let him lead me to the couch, where he sat and pulled me so that I straddled his lap.

He began caressing my breasts again. And I began to moan, biting my lip as his fingers teased my nipples to pinched pink points. They begged for his attention, and when he lowered his mouth to my nipples I gasped in pleasure, coming quickly.

He licked and sucked my nipple as if in no hurry to stop, and he pulled at the weight of my breasts balancing them in his hands. I moved my groin against his, shifting back and forth, rubbing my wetness against his body.

He couldn't feel it, but I could feel my wetness against my jeans. I wasn't used to this. I wasn't used to being so aroused. I had only been with one man, and he wasn't very inspiring in bed. My ex-husband.

Husband. That thought sent me spiraling into a sea of disdain and cut through the desire quickly. I was letting someone who was promised to another touch me in ways that even my ex-husband hadn't touched me.

I pushed his hands away before I could change my mind and stood, looking frantically for my shirt. What was wrong with me? I scrambled around looking for my shirt and trying not to feel like the world's biggest slut.

"Where is my stupid shirt?" I grumbled to myself as I fought back angry tears. I didn't even know why I was angry with Julius. I was a willing accomplice. Then it occurred to me that I wasn't upset with Julius, I was upset with myself.

Maybe that was the real reason I'd shown up. For this to happen. I tried not to think about that truth.

It was then that I noticed Julius standing there with my shirt in his hand looking a mix of bemused, amused, and guilty.

The guilty part made my head hurt.

"I'm sorry," I mumbled and grabbed the shirt from his hand. I placed it on quickly and turned to leave.

He didn't say a word. He just let me go.

I didn't know how I felt about that. I decided not to think about it as I walked out his door, trying not to cry. I didn't know what I felt worse about, that he didn't seem to care that I was leaving or that I had debased myself to that point.

It suddenly felt like what everyone had thought about me all those years ago was true. I was a home wrecker. I was a bad person. I couldn't even look at myself in the visor. I swallowed back more tears and swiped at the ones that were already running down my cheeks.

I didn't know what tomorrow held, but I promised myself that I would do better.

7

"Where are you? You're already late," the annoyed voice demanded to know. It was Claire, of course.

I couldn't get a break. That was what I got for not looking at my phone before answering it.

I stuttered, not sure what to say. Didn't she know already? Hadn't Julius told her the gig was up? Why was she calling, and why didn't she sound MORE pissed off?

"I... I...um—"

"I didn't know you had a stuttering problem. Anyway, hurry up and get here. Of course, I'm going to dock your pay for this."

As abruptly as she called, she disconnected. I felt like that was how Claire conducted all her phone calls and maybe her relationships too. Maybe that was why Ana was afraid of her.

I sat up confused. Not knowing what to do and still feeling sorry myself for what happened between Julius and me a few days ago.

I immediately stopped following him after the incident. And I expected to get a hate-filled message from Claire about my apparent incompetency. But that didn't happen, and I began to suspect that maybe he was deliberately keeping me in the dark. Maybe I was being ridiculous. He couldn't be that vindictive.

But what did I know? I didn't even know him. At one point, I thought he was a nice guy and then the other night happened. He probably could have easily said the same thing about me.

Sighing, I sat up and tried to figure out what to do. I planned to just sit around and not do anything. But then I got a text that succinctly told me that I would have to pay back all the money she gave me unless I was there in fifteen minutes flat.

Groaning, I tossed my phone with more force than I needed to and stomped into my bathroom, all the while trying to figure out what I would say when I got there… not just to Claire, but to Julius and Ana.

They loved each other. And I came in determined to ruin it. I was a prick.

I tossed on a dress and didn't bother doing my hair. I added some sandals and left the house.

My stomach was tight as I made the short trip to the location.

I still had the itinerary, so I knew where the next event was. I thought it was some sort of dinner party, or was it the wedding invitation redo. Who knew?

I didn't even bother to grab my camera, I realized, but I didn't expect to take any pictures. What was Julius waiting for? To humiliate me in front of everyone? Or maybe to humiliate his future mother-in law?

Claire was there as I climbed the steps to the lavish house, a modern monstrosity of angles and shapes and glass. But I kind of liked it. It was different.

"Finally"—she looked me over and shook her head—"came dressed to impress I see?"

I shrugged off her sarcastic comment and said that I had been in a hurry.

"No kidding. Did you at least remember your camera? That is your cover after all."

"It's in my purse," I lied. I didn't even have a purse.

"And where's your purse?"

"In the car," I lied again. Gosh, what was wrong with me? I was a semi-adulteress and a liar. I felt God wouldn't want to see me walking through the pearly gates. I was a disaster.

"Well go back and get it," she commanded and then smiled in the direction of someone to the left of me.

"Richard! You made it!" Then she turned back and growled at me, "Get that purse," before stomping away in the direction of her beloved Richard, whoever he was.

I turned to go back to my car, grateful that now I could just ditch the scene and never have to worry about Claire or Julius again.

And as my luck would have it, that was exactly who I ran into. Except he was with Ana. She was laughing at something he said, and they smiled at each other before noticing me.

Ana gave me a big smile and waved me over. She looked so happy. I was such an asshole.

"Hey, you made it. My mom was having a meltdown. I'm not sure why. There's nothing to take pictures of here except a bunch of old people eating food. Glad you're here anyway. Aren't we, Julius?"

Up until that point, I kept my eyes off his face. When I finally raised my eyes to meet his, I couldn't tell what he was thinking. I knew my face was the definition of guilt though.

He didn't answer her question and instead said, "I'm sure your mother is ecstatic that Becca finally made it."

"Oh oh, take her to that little set up in the back. That's a photographic moment just waiting to happen."

She walked away leaving us to awkwardly stare at each other in silence. I didn't know what to say and apparently, he didn't either. As far as I was concerned, he was a terrible person for cheating on Ana, and I was equally terrible for letting it happen. We were scum. I apparently attracted that kind. First Tom and now Julius. I was starting to think maybe I was the reason guys behaved so terribly. Maybe something about me just said that I was open to being the other woman. But I wasn't. I wasn't going to be the other woman.

I scanned my surroundings and saw that no one was around, and I opened my mouth to tell him exactly that. Incidentally, we both started talking at the same time.

"I'm sorry—" we both said and then paused awkwardly. It was hard to meet his eyes. I couldn't do it. So I stared at the ground and dug a hole with the tip of my shoe to distract myself from feeling something I wasn't allowed to feel.

"I think we're sorry for different things."

I looked up then. That comment was unexpected. So what exactly was he apologizing for?

"I take it your mother-in-law and Ana don't know what happened the other night."

"Yep, and I'd like to keep it that way—"

"Is that why you haven't exposed that I'm not just a photographer?"

"Pretty much."

"So by saving my hide, you save your own." God, I sure knew how to pick them.

"Kind of."

We stared at each other in silence and then he finally said, "I guess you need to go get your camera.

"Yeah…"

"Okay. Meet you out back in ten minutes."

He walked away toward the area Ana disappeared to, and I sighed. My cover wouldn't be blown, but wasn't it wrong to just play along? Now I was deceiving everyone around me, except Julius. He knew the real me. He knew way too much.

I didn't do vulnerability well.

I was torn between being disgusted over what I had done to blaming Julius for it all. He didn't seem to feel guilty at all. Had I stumbled into another situation where I was dating a man without a conscience? It certainly seemed that way, and I wasn't even dating the guy. He was about to get married. I felt like I was the worst. And I felt terrible for Ana.

I knew I didn't have the courage to tell her what happened. I was a coward, and I didn't know how she would respond. What if she tried to clobber me with a champagne bottle or something? What if, even worse, she just started sobbing? No, I couldn't do that to her. I didn't want her to know what type of person I truly was. I had sunk to a new low, an unforgivable low.

Feeling dejected and sad, my shoulders slumped. I just had to make sure nothing like what happened the other night happened again. Determined, I walked to my car to retrieve my purse.

I ended up taking pictures with my phone and reassuring Claire that I would just use Photoshop to make sure the pictures came out looking great. It was almost as if she forgot that I wasn't really there to photograph everything.

I wasn't sure why she cared; it wasn't like she would show them to anybody. After all, she didn't want them to get married.

I didn't know how I felt about that. I knew it wasn't my call to make. Did Claire have a valid reason for not wanting Julius with her daughter? After all, I had first-hand knowledge that he wasn't completely faithful. Maybe Julius was a womanizer. What would've happened if I hadn't stopped him that day at his home?

Something inside me didn't want to believe that Julius was a bad guy. But he had to be, right? I wasn't entirely to blame, nor was he, but he had more to lose, more at stake. He hadn't invited me over. He hadn't invited me in. I created that situation. And there was no denying that I was attracted to him from the start. But he was taken, and I needed to constantly remind myself of that.

We were both to blame, but I had a feeling that more of that blame fell on me. God, I had issues.

When the brunch or whatever it was ended, I made my way to the car, only to see Julius leaning against it.

"We need to talk," he said, not bothering to move.

"No… we don't need to talk." I had already decided that I would never be alone with him again since it appeared that I couldn't control myself or my actions when Julius was involved.

"Yeah, we do."

"Get off my car." I tried to sound intimidating, but my voice shook, belying my false fierceness. To my surprise, though, he stepped away from my door.

"Go away before someone sees you talking to me," I hissed as I pulled the door open and climbed in.

He seemed unconcerned and closed my door for me before continuing. "If someone sees us talking, they'll just assume I have questions for you. No biggie. But we do need to talk, clear the air—"

"Nope," I said, putting the key in the ignition.

"Come on, Becca."

"Don't come on Becca me. We need to be far, far away from each other." I rubbed a frustrated hand through my hair. "Look at what we did. We were pawing at each other like sex-crazed bunnies. You're getting married, and look at what we're doing," I harshly whispered to him.

"I'm not getting married."

I was stunned. Oh no. Oh no. What had I done?

"No, no, no… you're getting married, mister."

He gave a small smile. "No, I'm not. And by the way, I like it when you're trying to sound tough. It's cute."

I ignored his comment and found it kind of lame. "You can't… you can't do this to Ana. You can't."

He looked taken aback. "Do this to Ana? She's the one who told me to go for it."

Now it was my turn to look taken aback. "I'm sorry. I'm just having a hard time digesting what you just said. So you think she would be okay with her future husband having sex with other women?"

"It's not… We're not"—he paused and tried again—"Ana's my friend, but our relationship isn't exactly how you believe it to be."

"Oh my gosh… are you guys swingers? Ana looks way too sweet for that…"

He laughed, but I ignored him and kept talking, "You guys are, aren't you? I should have known."

He opened his mouth, but I continued to talk, not giving him the opportunity to confirm or deny what I had guessed.

"Are you guys one of those open marriage couples?

I knew there was a lot of judgement in my tone, and although I was in no position to judge that didn't stop me. He didn't respond; instead, he got really close to me, just within kissing distance, and plucked something out of my hair.

I laughed nervously and tried to move away. He easily blocked me and reached down and grabbed me by my chin. "You're wrong. Is that a good enough answer?"

I shook my head, but the way he was looking at me made me want to reconsider my response. Snap out of it, my conscience shouted at me.

"Listen, I'm sorry. I can't do this." I pulled away, and he jumped back quickly trying to avoid the wheels of my car.

I heard him swear, and I felt bad and yelled sorry from the window as I drove away.

I had almost run him over, but he kind of deserved it. He wasn't going to marry Ana? Oh God, what had I done?

* * *

I WOKE up from a much-needed nap. I got out of bed feeling like a lazy person for sleeping in the middle of the day. I felt groggy, and my heart hurt. I thought it was because of guilt. I spent the past weekend taking pictures and trying my best to not be alone with Julius. I exhausted me. If it weren't for the fact that I needed the money, I would have quit a long time ago.

I made my way to the kitchen, wondering where my dad was. I didn't see him inside and just shrugged it off and sat in front of the TV. I couldn't believe it. I had the

TV to myself. I reached for the remote, hoping to binge watch a superhero drama on Netflix when I heard my dad talking to someone.

Being nosy, I got up and looked out the window. I'd bet it was his lady love. Apparently, he hit it off with the school librarian, a woman named Lori. They were suddenly an item. I met her and liked her. She had a ton of energy and made my dad seem more alive.

Dad was old and had found love again. I was young and still crap at it. I peered through the window then screamed and jumped out of sight. My dad was talking to Julius. One, how did Julius know where I lived and two, why was he here? And most importantly, number three, did he hear me scream and jump from in front of the window like a crazy person?

I rushed to the bathroom and brushed my teeth. Added a little extra deodorant and tried to do something with my hair. It was at an awkward length, so there wasn't much I could do. I briefly thought about putting on a hairband, but I was told that I resembled a Disney princess so I didn't want the headband to make me look even more cartoonish.

I looked down and tried to rub the stain off my shirt. It was orange as if I had been eating chips. I groaned to myself. I had been eating chips. I went to pull it off when I remembered it was the only clean shirt I had since I hated doing laundry. I scrubbed at it with a piece of tissue and only made it worse. Now I had a huge orange stain and little pieces of tissue stuck to it. It was yucky, but there was nothing I could do.

Thinking quickly, I went back to my room, grabbed a jacket and tied it around my waist.

I inspected myself in the mirror and tried not to groan. I looked like a 1990s boyband member that my mother was so fond of. But hey, it would hide the huge stain. Sighing, I realized that I really didn't know when to quit. My life was like the huge stain on my shirt. If I had just left well enough alone I wouldn't be such a mess.

My father and Julius were in the kitchen when I came out. They looked up at me at the same time.

"New look?" my dad asked with a smirk as he checked out my jacket. I rolled my eyes just like a teenager and sort of felt like one again. I didn't want my dad talking to Julius. That sounded embarrassing. Who knew what he'd probably already told him…

And then I saw it, a photo album. He was showing Julius my baby pictures.

I walked over and snatched the book up. "Seriously, Dad?!"

"What?" he said with a light shrug. "You were a cute baby, and you never invite anyone over so I never have anyone to share them with."

"That's a good thing."

"You're the first friend she's brought over in a while. I was beginning to think she didn't have any," my dad said with a grin.

"Dad, seriously, come on."

"What?"

"You're embarrassing me and making me look like a lonely, friendless old lady."

"If the shoe fits..." Julius added to the conversation, letting his voice trail off. Now I wanted to hit him. I was being double team, and I didn't like it.

I put my hands on my hips and turned my ire in Julius' direction first.

"What are you doing here?" I demanded.

"Uh oh... someone's cranky," Dad laughed.

"And when did you become such a comedian?" I folded my arms over my chest, trying to look mean.

I failed apparently because my dad said, "She used to pout just like that when she was a little girl. In fact, I think I might have a picture..."

Dad got up and started wandering through the house in search of a picture of me. I rolled my eyes and turned in Julius' direction.

"What's wrong with you?"

"What?"

"You're practically stalking me. I told you that I didn't want to be alone with you."

"We're not alone... your dad is right here."

"You know what I meant."

"Maybe I didn't."

"Don't play stupid."

"I have no idea what you're talking about."

"I'm talking about you showing up here, uninvited and bewitching my dad. You're like a charismatic stalker."

"Thanks… I think."

"That was supposed to be an insult, not a compliment. Stalking people isn't okay."

"Oh you mean, like how you followed me around for days on end? So you're saying that's not okay?"

I narrowed my eyes at him. "That was the job."

"So it's okay to stalk people for money, but anything else is just wrong?"

"Yes," I said, feeling stuck in a corner.

"That doesn't make any sense."

"You don't make any sense."

He smiled at me and reached for my hand. "I think we just had our first official fight as a couple."

I snatched my hand back and looked around, wondering where Dad had gone. Our condo wasn't that big. "We're not fighting and most importantly, we're not a couple."

"Whatever you say, sweetheart."

"Don't call me sweetheart."

"Sure, babe."

I wanted to strangle him, but I forced myself to take a deep breath. I wasn't going to let him get a rise out of me.

"So, stalker, why are you here?"

He shrugged. "I was in the neighborhood and figured I'd stop by."

"You just happened to be in my neighborhood? Nearly an hour away from where you live? You really expect me to believe that?"

He shrugged. "It was worth a shot."

I couldn't help but laugh.

"Finally, a smile," he said, and my heart went pitter-patter. My stupid heart.

"I know this is kind of a weird move—"

"Kind of?"

"But if you won't spend time with me, then I'll spend time with you."

"You know it doesn't work that way, right?"

He shrugged yet again. "I'm open to trying something new. What about you?"

I wanted to say yes. So much so that it scared me. And for that reason, I knew what I had to do.

"I can't see you, Julius. You're getting married."

"I told you—"

"Stop. Just stop talking. I'm not... I won't... I can't be that person. This is all wrong."

"Becca—"

"No. You have to leave."

"Is that what you really want?"

No. Definitely not. That wasn't what I wanted. I wanted him to hold me, kiss me, and touch me. I wanted to know him better. Where did he grow up? Who were his friends? I wanted to know everything and more about this man. But this man was already taken, first and foremost.

And so I lied, "Yes. That's what I really want."

I immediately felt terrible.

"You're a bad liar," he said, standing up. "But you win… at least for now."

I didn't know how to respond, so I just looked down at my toes.

"Leaving already," my dad asked Julius, suddenly appearing from out of nowhere.

"Yeah, I have a meeting on the other side of town."

"That's too bad." Dad held out his hand, and Julius shook it.

"See you later, Becca."

"Bye," I said softly as he left.

When he closed the door behind him, my dad locked it and then turned to me and said, "He's a keeper, that one."

"Dad, you don't even know him."

"I know a winner when I meet one. You guys would be great together."

"He's—" I was about to say getting married, but I didn't want Dad's opinion of me to be darkened by that truth. I was his saintly Becca. And I wanted to keep it that way.

"He's what?"

"He's my client. And I don't get involved with clients…"

"Since when did you start having client—"

"Recently," I lied, feeling a teeny bit guilty. "I do more than just photograph cheaters, Dad."

"Good for you," he said, meaning it. He always wanted so much for me, and I felt like an absolute disappointment. I'd done nothing with my degree. I had a dead end job. There was so much I needed to work on. And getting involved with an almost married man wasn't going to help.

"Since you're awake, want to play a game of cards?"

"Sure," I said, taking a seat at the table.

When the day eventually turned to night, I told my dad that I needed to get some work done. That wasn't exactly true. I just needed space and some time to think.

My life felt like it was going nowhere fast. And I had no clue how to change it.

THE NEXT DAY I met up with Meredith, Piper, and Dana for lunch. It was a burrito bar and Dana kept talking about all the calories, but was the one who got the most stuff.

"You guys are making it really hard to be on a diet," she said.

"Diets are a waste of time," Piper chimed in.

"Piper, you could eat candy bars and pizza every day and not gain a pound, so spare me."

I was used to Dana and Piper arguing. It seemed to be just how they communicated. It was clear that they were best friends. I felt privileged to be part of their inner circle. I learned a lot about them over the years. They helped me grow up, which sounded kind of funny to admit. It was hard to believe I was so young when we first met. And now they were a huge part of my life. I considered them my best friends. So why then had I not told them about Julius? But then again, there wasn't anything to tell, right?

"Ladies, I need your help. My life is all upside down. What should I do?"

I took them by surprise, clearly. They just shot me puzzled looks. "Exactly what is upside down?" Piper asked before taking a bite of her burrito.

She closed her eyes and moaned in pleasure. "This is so, so good."

Dana and I laughed.

"I need a career. I have a degree that I worked really hard for, but yet, I'm not doing anything with it."

"You're preaching to the choir. I didn't do anything with my degree for like a decade," Dana said. She was a stay at home mom and hadn't started working until after she was divorced.

"Oh gosh, I don't want that to happen to me."

Piper almost choked on her burrito, and her eyes were filled with laughter. Dana, on the other hand, didn't look as amused.

"Sorry," I said, feeling really badly. "I mean… there was nothing wrong with what you did. I just don't have an excuse. I'm not raising a baby or running a household…"

"Or still married to a chauvinist," Dana added in happily.

"What's a chauvinist?" Meredith asked.

"Nothing, hon. Mom's just being testy again."

Meredith shrugged her shoulders as if fine with that answer and started to eat, humming as she did. She was just so cute.

"I think I should be doing more with my life, you know?"

"Well, why don't you do something with those photography skills you have?"

"I am doing something."

Everyone stopped eating and gave me a look.

"Hey, it pays the bills," I said in my defense, knowing what they all were thinking.

"Paying the bills is great and all, but you're too young to not follow your passion. You earned a bachelor's degree and that's great. But photography is your love. You should do something with that," Piper said helpfully.

"Yeah, but what?"

"I can set up a website for you," Dana offered. "A real one." She was a marketing genius. She went from barely knowing what Twitter was to managing several Twitter accounts and other social media pages for not only her company but also a few side gigs. She was getting paid pretty well for it. I was proud of her.

"That would be great, but how do I get clients?"

"That's my specialty," Piper said. She ran a really profitable translation business that spanned the globe last time I had heard.

"We can come up with a business plan, if you want," Piper continued. "And I can give you some ideas for recruiting clients, especially those who are abroad."

"That would be so amazing," I said, feeling honored and touched by their kindness.

"It's a plan then."

We hashed out the rest of the details while we ate, and when we were done I was feeling a sense of accomplishment. Maybe my love life was going nowhere fast, but at least I was getting my career in order.

After lunch, I headed home only to find Julius there again.

"What are you doing here?" I said as he got out of his car and followed me to the door of my condo.

"I just came over to play chess with Mrs. Nguyen."

"Stop talking to my neighbors."

"Well, you won't talk to me. I have to talk to someone."

"Why won't you just go away?"

"I will, after you hear me out."

"No thanks."

"Have it your way. I guess you'll just have to endure these little visits from me on the daily basis."

Something told me that his words weren't an empty threat.

Sighing, I unlocked the door and pushed it open. I called out to Dad and then remembered that he was at Lori's. That meant I was alone with Julius. Oh no. What had I done?

I motioned for him to take a seat at the table. "Okay, you have two minutes…"

"This sounds familiar."

I wanted to just say forget it all and give in. But I was better than that. At least I was trying to be better than that.

"Julius, you need to stop coming over."

"You need to stop being so stubborn."

He took my hands in his. "I've missed you lately. Life isn't the same without you following me around wearing a very hideous wig."

I fought the smile that threatened to expose me.

"Go ahead," he said, still holding my hands. "Show me that pretty smile of yours. I've missed that the most."

"Julius, we can't do this. You shouldn't be here."

"Who are you trying to convince? Me? Or yourself?"

He didn't wait for me to respond. He simply pushed the plastic table out of the way between us and pulled me in his arms.

I wanted to protest. I wanted to push him away, but I couldn't bring myself to move. Being in Julius' arms was where I wanted to be. I told myself that I would just let him hold me for just a moment or two. What harm was a moment?

And so he held me, initiating nothing. Just holding me against his chest. I sighed and confessed, "I could stay like this forever."

"And I would love to hold you like this… forever."

I knew I had to pull away. I had to end this, but my body wasn't cooperating. I wasn't sure who moved first; it was probably me. But one moment I was in his lap, just sitting there and the next, my arms were wrapped around his neck and my lips were on his.

I wanted him badly. The other night was still in my head. It was as if our night together had only whet my appetite for him. We stumbled into my bedroom, and I found suddenly that I was the aggressor.

I lowered myself to my knees and unzipped his pants. I yearned to taste him. He was clearly ready for me. He was long and hard and thick just like I knew he would be. I pulled his member into my mouth, taking in only the tip and sucking at the drop of desire I found there. He sighed and buried his hands in my hair, keeping my mouth on his sex as he pushed his hips forward, forcing me to take more of him in. I greedily opened my mouth wider to accommodate the size of him. I licked and sucked his sex, bringing my head back as far as Julius would let me before bringing the fullness of him into my mouth.

I could feel that he was about to come. He let go of my head, and I pulled back just enough to release him from my mouth and then I sucked gently on the head. He came then, and I pulled my mouth away and worked his sex with my hand, enjoying the feel of his member as he came hard, gasping my name. I let him come on my chest, rubbing his member in between my breasts.

He removed his shirt and cleaned me up.

"It's my turn," he said, pulling me up. He quickly undressed me from the waist down, pushing my panties down around my ankles then turned me around. He made me brace my hands against the wall, and I groaned as he parted my folds from behind. He stuck his finger in my sex, and greedily my sex tightened around his finger. He stuck another one in and then another, stretching my sex as he played in my wetness.

"God you taste good," he groaned, licking his fingers that were covered by my wetness. I bent over lower and spread my legs even further. I needed him in me and was trying to give him as much access as possible.

In the darkness of the room, he slid his hand up my shirt and began to play with my nipples. I moaned against him and rubbed my behind against his crotch. He didn't wait for an invitation as he buried his head between my legs. I gasped as he pushed his tongue inside of me. He wasn't gentle. He was rough, taking what he wanted as I tried to hold back a scream.

I covered my mouth but still cried out as he traced his tongue up my folds, licking at my wetness. I couldn't take it anymore. I needed him inside me.

"Please," I gasped as he spread my legs even more and penetrated me with his tongue.

"What do you want?"

"You," I gasped.

He pulled away and took me from behind, grabbing hold of my hips to pull me back to meet every one of his thrusts.

He pounded into me with wild abandon. Pushing

into me, filling me with his hard, smooth, thickness. I needed more and spread my legs, hoping that would give him better access. I came then, unexpectedly. My whole body shook, and my inner muscles tensed around his sex. I felt one with him as my sex molded to his. But he wasn't done yet. He placed his hand between us, caressing my clit as he moved his throbbing sex in and out of me.

I shook as I came again. "Julius!" I yelled, over and over as waves of pleasure radiated from my clit to the rest of me. I shouted his name until I was hoarse. Sweat trickled down my face, and I gasped for air. He slowed down and was teasing me with his thrusts, pushing inside of me just enough to make my hips jerk in anticipation.

He was torturing me with his dick, not giving me all that I wanted, enjoying the way I squirmed for more.

"Julius, please," I begged as he slid just the head into me. My hips pushed back, greedy for more. I needed all of him.

And finally, he complied, sliding the length of his sex inside me. "Better?" he teased.

"God yes," I sighed, only to scream a moment later as he started to play with my clit yet again.

It was his turn to groan as I came hard, my sex caressing his dick, spasm after spasm, squeezing and clenching around his sex. I felt him come then, shouting my name this time as he bucked against me, spilling his cum deep inside my warmth.

We stayed in that position for a few minutes trying to catch our breath when I heard from the distance Mrs. Nguyen call out to my father.

I instantly froze up, and I could feel Julius do the same. He pulled out of me, and we stumbled around for our clothes.

Julius looked for an escape, and I gestured to my bedroom window.

"You have got to be kidding me."

"Go!" I yelled, tossing his keys to him that had fallen from his pants pocket.

"We're adults!" he protested as I pushed him through the window.

"Tell that to my dad," I whispered loudly as I raced away from my bedroom window and through the living room. I was so thankful that Mrs. Nguyen was a talker. I fixed the table and then jumped into the shower.

"Please don't let him suspect anything. Please… please…" I said to myself as I scrubbed away the scent of Julius' lovemaking from my body.

Yes, I was an adult, but I couldn't bear the thought of my dad knowing what I was just up to.

A few minutes later, I was clean, dry, and dressed.

Dad was sitting at the table whistling. "Why are you so happy?" I said, rummaging through the pantry for something to eat. I grabbed a box of cereal and started eating directly out of the box. I was starving suddenly. I guess rambunctious, midday sex could do that to you.

He held up a letter. "This is the last hospital bill. Officially done," he said, sending me a big smile.

I hugged him. "That's great, Dad. You and Lori should go out somewhere to celebrate."

He nodded. "That's a good idea. You should come too. And Julius, if he wants."

I shook my head and tried not to blush at the sound of Julius' name. "I'm sure he's busy," I mumbled, stuffing my mouth with cereal.

"Really?" Dad held up something that looked exactly like Julius' wallet. I could feel myself turning red. "Next time Julius decides to go sneaking out windows, remind him to at least NOT leave his wallet on the floor."

He tossed me the wallet, and I caught it. Dad laughed, ruffled my hair and got on the phone with Lori.

I groaned and shut myself in my room.

"There you are," a voice said from the window. "I think Mrs. Nguyen is getting suspicious. Have you seen my wallet?"

I stared at Julius in shock. He was still outside my bedroom window. At least he was fully dressed,. "What are you still doing here?"

"I left my wallet. I can't drive without my wallet."

I tossed it to him. "Now go home," I hissed.

"I'll call you later," he promised.

"I won't answer."

He winked at me. "Yes, you will."

He blew me a kiss and scrambled away. I watched him leave with a smile on my face that slowly faded as I thought of the enormity of what we had done. How could something feel so right but be so wrong?

8

There was determination in my steps as I made my way to the entrance of Claire's home. Her home was located in a rich gated community clear across town from where I lived. The gatekeeper readily waved me in having seen me several times already.

I decided to give myself a break and unplug for the weekend. It was what I needed to do before I had to tell Ana the truth.

I decided that I was going to just walk up to her and tell her. I was going to tell her that I betrayed her trust in more ways than one. It was going to be hard, but I couldn't keep lying to her. She was the innocent one in all this. I didn't care that Julius tried to convince me that she would be okay with us seeing each other. I didn't believe him. No woman was okay with sharing a man. As far as I was concerned, that just wasn't the way the world worked.

And even if she was okay with it, I wouldn't be. I wasn't going to share Julius with Ana. I simply couldn't. I loved him too much to share him with anyone.

First, I would start with Claire. "I'm done lying, Claire. I quit," I said as soon I saw her. Thankfully, she was alone and just getting off the phone with someone.

She barely glanced at me. "Fine. I don't need you anymore anyway. I have what I need."

What did she mean by that? And why wasn't she upset? Wasn't this her cue to throw a tantrum and threaten me? Why was she so calm about it?

"What are you talking about? What do you mean, you have what you need?" She couldn't possibly know about what was going on between me and Julius. God, I hoped she didn't. But the look on her face, that smirk, made me think otherwise.

She shook her head. "It was all so easy. Tell me something: did you fall into bed with him the first minute you met him, or did you at least wait a few hours?"

My mouth fell open, and my stomach churned. I was caught between shock and utter disbelief.

I was speechless, but Claire wasn't. "You're disgusting… almost as bad as he is."

I was shocked by her words, and tears welled up in my eyes. "How dare you?"

"Don't you dare pretend to be virtuous and sweet! I know what you've done!"

"Mom, Becca, what's going on here?" Ana came into the study and looked from me to her mother.

Calmly, her mother pulled an envelope out of her desk and handed it to Ana.

"Ana, I'm sorry to hurt you, but you need to see these."

I frowned, wondering what she had to show her. Her eyes seemed victorious. What exactly had she won? Why was she looking so smug?

Ana pulled the contents out of the envelope and her face tensed in disgust.

She tossed the envelope on the desk in front of her and looked up at her mother, her face showing an emotion I wouldn't have recognized if I hadn't looked at my own mother that way so long ago. It was hate.

"How dare you?"

"What?"

"How dare you?" Ana said again, furiously knocking the pictures off her mother's desk to the floor. "What did you do? Did you seriously hire someone to follow him around? To invade our privacy?"

"I did what I had to do," Claire said, clearly surprised that Ana's anger was directed toward her.

"What you had to do?" Ana's tone was venomous.

It was then that Julius walked in.

"What's going on in here?"

"What's going on is that it's over, Julius. There's no way Ana will marry you now."

He looked from Claire to Ana. "Ana, what is your mom talking about?"

"She hired someone to follow you. Take a look." Ana gestured toward the envelope now on the floor. He bent down and looked at the pictures that spilled from the envelope.

"Wow… you stooped to a new low, Mom."

I was confused. What were the pictures of? I hadn't given her any pictures. At least not any pictures that were incriminating.

I reached for the envelope. There were pictures of me leaving his home. There were pictures of us walking together. There were pictures of us embracing. And then there were others not so innocent. Someone had gotten quite a few shots of us of that night I visited him in his home. There were pictures of us kissing. There were pictures of me in various stages of undress. And then there was a very telling picture of both of us looking disheveled and satiated. There were others of us. Lots of others.

Who had taken them?

"How did you get these?" I asked, finding my voice.

"Your boss."

It all made perfect sense now. I remembered running into her at the park while I was following Julius. I remembered thinking how nonchalant she was about me taking on fewer clients. Because the whole time I thought I was following Julius, she was actually following me.

"But how?"

"Oh please, stop playing innocent. I knew he was attracted to you when I saw how pushy he was about paying you that day at the botanical garden. And I wasn't surprised. At all. All guys fall for the doe-eyed blonde. It was only a matter of time, so I had your boss tail you until it happened."

I felt sick. She deceived me, and I played straight into her hands.

I wanted to disappear. I had to get air. I had to get away from her. This was insanity. It was one thing to know that Ana didn't care about what happened between Julius and me, but it was another for her mom to know what happened too. I was humiliated. It made me feel dirty. I felt like a whore. She was right about me. It had been only a matter of time before Julius and I slept together.

I went to leave when Ana grabbed my arm catching me by surprise. The steely look in her eyes made her practically unrecognizable.

It was a look her mother definitely mastered.

"Don't leave, Becca. You're not at fault here. You're a real class act, Mom. A real class act." Her voice was low and vicious.

Claire looked shocked. Now she was the one at a loss for words.

"What? Are you angry with me? I'm not the one who cheated—" Her voice cracked, and she tried to regain her composure. "How dare you take that tone with me, young lady? I only did what was best for you."

"What was best for me? Setting up my fiancé? Violating his privacy? That's what was best for me?"

"None of this is my fault. He made the decision to pursue her; I just provided the means." She sounded so self-satisfied. But she was right. So right about me. I made it easy.

"I knew Becca and Julius were seeing each other, Mom."

Claire shook her head, not understanding.

"And you still planned to marry him?" she said with her voice full of disgust.

"That's just it, Mom, I never planned to marry him."

"What? What are you even talking about? This is insane."

"No! That's what I've been trying to tell you for years: You're insane."

"Watch your words, young lady. I am your mother!"

"And that's what makes what you did so despicable."

"What I did? What about what he did?"

"Are you even listening to me? What is your problem? This was never about me or Julius. He was just being my friend, saving me from dealing with you on my own."

"You're not making any sense."

"You kept going on and on about how I needed to choose a career. Make something of myself. Settle down. Etcetera, etcetera. Nothing I did was ever good enough. Where I went to college, my career, who I loved..."

Claire laughed hoarsely, "Being someone's secretary is not a career."

"You see!" Anne cried out, her voice breaking. "You're still doing it. Even now. You're still trying to make me feel bad."

"I'm not trying to make you feel bad. I'm trying to get you to live up to your potential. I just want you to be somebody."

"Instead of a nobody, right?" Ana said, sounding dejected.

"I never said that."

"You didn't have to." Ana wiped away at a tear.

"So this whole marriage thing was just a sham? A lie? Did you put her up to this?" She looked accusingly at Julius.

"He didn't put me up to anything, Mom. This was all

my doing. I didn't want to disappoint you again, and when you went on and on about how your best friend's daughter was getting married, I just lied and said I was too. It was silly and stupid. But for a moment, you seemed to be actually happy for me, and it felt good to see you actually supportive of me. To see you pay attention to me."

"Are you kidding me? What are you? Two? You're lying now to get attention. God this is humiliating. What am I going to tell people?"

"What are you going to tell people? Oh my God, Mom, why is everything about you?"

Claire sent Ana a venomous look. "Oh please. I gave you everything, absolutely everything a kid could want, and this is how you repay me? With lies? My whole life was about you, making you happy, making sure you were provided for. I built an empire for you. So stop with the tears. You don't know anything about what I sacrificed for you. And for what? For you to become some secretary and apparently some sort of compulsive liar. I'm not taking the blame because you can't figure out how to be an adult."

The silence after that statement was deafening. My heart ached for Ana. Even my own mother wouldn't have gone so far.

"You're right. I have no one to blame but myself. And it's time for me to start behaving like an adult. You're right, Mom. So I'm going to do the adult thing and ask you to get out of my life. Actually, don't bother. I'll just stay out of yours. I'm done being your daughter."

"It doesn't work like that," Claire said, finally sounding unsure.

"No, it does," Ana said with utmost certainty. "Stay out of my life, and I'll stay out of yours. I'm sorry your sacrifice didn't pay off. But hey, at least you have that empire that you built to comfort you; it'll be more of a legacy than I could have ever lived to be."

And with that, Ana walked away. Claire didn't try to stop her. She just watched her go, her mouth pulling into a tight line. She turned her eyes to us and looked thunderous.

"Do you see what you have done?"

Julius shook his head. "What I've done? Your adult daughter was pretending to get married to please you, to make you happy, and you're blaming me?"

Claire shook her head. "Get out of my house. Both of you. Get out of here." She then growled at me, "And I expect all my money back from you."

"Not a chance in hell," Julius said, sticking up for me.

"Try me," she said.

I knew Julius wasn't done fighting, but I was as I pulled at his sleeve. "Let's go. It's not worth it, Julius."

He didn't break eye contact with Claire. "You just lost your daughter, Claire. Instead of trying to figure out how to hurt us, why don't you figure out how to be a mother?"

And with that, he took my hand and we left the house. There was no sign of Ana outside. She was gone.

I was still reeling from being used as bait. I felt dirty. What had she seen when she looked at me? Someone without morals? How could she have been so sure that he would go for me and that I would let him? How could she had known me so much better than I knew myself?

"What's wrong?" Julius asked, touching my chin and bringing my face up to meet his eyes.

"I just... I fell straight into her trap. It's like she knew I wouldn't say no to a married man."

"It wasn't real, Becca. I never planned to marry Ana."

"I know that," I said, stepping away from his touch. Suddenly, it made me feel dirty. "But I didn't know that at the beginning when we kissed. I was attracted to you right from the start, and I shouldn't have let those feelings develop."

"Becca."

"No, she was ultimately right about me... about us."

"No she wasn't. You didn't do anything wrong, Becca."

"Didn't I? I went to your place that night and if we hadn't stopped, I would have willingly slept with you when I knew you were supposed to marry another.

What does that say about me, Julius? What kind of person does that make me?"

"Becca, stop, nothing happened that night."

"But I would have let something happen. And that's the point." I turned away from him and walked over to my car. He grabbed my hand, trying to stop me.

"Becca, let's talk about this."

"There's nothing to talk about. I just need to be alone right now. I'll call you."

He let go of my hand and didn't say another word, but I could tell there was more he wanted to say, more he wanted to do, but I wasn't ready to listen.

"Promise me you'll call."

"I promise," was all I said, not looking at him as I climbed behind the wheel and started the car.

I drove away, not bothering to look behind me. I didn't want to see him. I didn't want to think of how I was hurting him. I felt that I was actually running away. Running away from being loved...

I needed to get far away from him. I needed to get far away from everything. The whole situation made me feel uncertain... dirty even.

I wandered briefly if even now my boss was following me. Feeling emboldened, I reached for my phone and called her.

"Becca? What's up? You need another assignment?"

"I know what you did, Leona."

"What?"

"Don't try to deny it. Claire told us that you've been following Julius and me around."

"Claire needs to learn to keep her mouth shut, but a job's a job, right?"

I didn't bother to answer. I hung up and texted her that I quit. But didn't I feel the same way? Didn't I take the job just because Claire promised me so much money? Didn't I follow Julius around and violate his privacy? Didn't I at least in the very beginning betray Ana's and Julius' trust? So who was I to judge?

I didn't even recognize myself. Who did I become?

An hour later, I parked in front of my dad's condo and frowned at the spot that was normally reserved for Mrs. Nguyen's granddaughter. I didn't recognize the car that was parked there now. Mrs. Nguyen normally let us use it if we ever had guests over. Dad had a guest? Great. Just great. Now was not the time that I wanted to be social. I walked up the driveway, past the courtyard, and inserted my key in the lock. The door wasn't even closed, I realized.

"Dad, you forgot to lock the door," I called and then to my shock I saw my dad on his knees with Lori in front of him. And a ring in his hand.

"Oh my god! I'm so sorry!" I said, clearly shocked. My dad was proposing to Lori. Didn't he just meet her like yesterday? What was going on in the world?

"No, no, no. Don't be," Lori said, snatching the ring from his hand. "I'm just glad you were able to see such a monumental... well, moment... Yes! Yes! Yes, Phil! I'll marry you!"

My dad tried to stand up, but he was a little off balance, so Lori helped him. He shouldn't have been kneeling on his bad knee, I thought to myself, completely forgetting the romance of it all.

"Oh, Becca, can you believe it? Can you really believe it? It's happening. It's really happening."

Lori looked more like a retired Las Vegas showgirl than a librarian, in my opinion. She had deep-set almond-shaped, gray eyes and jet black hair that hung to her waist. She was well-endowed up top and wore very low cut shirts that seemed to magnify the size of her cleavage. I think Dad said she was half-Albanian and half-Egyptian. I honestly couldn't remember. She was a knockout and knocking on her early sixties. And did I mention, she was seriously the sweetest most excitable lady I knew?

I tightly smiled. My life was imploding around me. I didn't know where I stood with Julius. And now I was going to have a stepmom? Life just needed to slow down. I couldn't keep up, and I wasn't sure if I actually wanted to.

Now Lori was holding me in a vice grip, hugging the

life out of me. She was only four-feet-eleven, but strong for such a petite woman.

"Now it's time for some champagne!" She turned to my father. "Did you get champagne?"

He looked caught off guard. "Was I supposed to?"

Lori laughed, "I love you so much. I'll get the champagne. Be right back, you guys." And with that, Lori disappeared out the door.

I watched her go still kind of shell-shocked myself.

Dad was rubbing his knee and looking at me strangely.

"You okay?" he asked.

"Yeah."

"You don't look like it."

"I guess I'm just shocked, that's all."

"I know it's sudden."

"Yeah," I said again. Boy, I wasn't very articulate lately.

His face fell. "You're not happy for me?"

I immediately felt terrible and went over to my dad and gave him a big hug.

"Dad, of course I'm happy for you. Lori's great."

"I know this is sudden."

"No... I mean... yeah... but it's, you know, your decision."

He nodded. "I know. I just want you to be happy for me. You know?"

"Dad, I promise you, I am happy for you. I think Lori is wonderful. Crazy, but wonderful."

He laughed, "She's great. She keeps me on my toes." He cleared his throat. "Lori and I have been talking about moving in together and I just felt like, why not go all the way?"

"You guys are moving in together?"

"Yeah, not soon, after you find your own place."

Oh god, I needed to find my own place. My mind was reeling. I was going to be homeless and loveless.

I held back a pitiful moan.

"Are you okay?"

I sat heavily on the couch and put my head between my legs and tried to breathe since I felt like I was having a panic attack.

My heartbeat was racing. My mind was racing. Random thoughts were popping up. I felt like I was going to faint. God, I was so dramatic.

"Just breathe. You're not having some sort of heart attack, are you? According to the news, a heart attack can happen to anyone."

"I'm not having a heart attack, Dad."

"Huh?"

I realized that my head was still down and I was mumbling. Of course he didn't understand a word I said.

"I was saying that I'm not having a heart attack,"

Tears welled up in my eyes then. "I'm just so disappointed with myself."

And then I started to sob.

Dad just held me, not knowing what I was crying about but not giving up on me. He was a great father. I was a terrible daughter and started crying harder at the thought.

"Hey, hey, hush… you're fine. It's okay."

I felt like I was seven again, but I didn't care. I let myself be comforted. I needed it.

Finally, when I didn't have any more tears to cry, I raised my head.

"So you're going to tell me what that was all about? I'm sure you're not that broken up over me getting married."

I wiped at my nose, and my dad reached for a paper towel from the kitchen and handed it to me.

"No, it's not that at all. I just… I'm a disaster at love."

"What are you talking about?"

"I messed up, Dad." I wiped at another stray tear.

"Tell me what happened." I filled him in, leaving out the really personal parts.

He listened patiently, not interrupting.

"Wow, that's quite a doozey. So Julius was supposed to be getting married, but wasn't really. And you two fell for each other. And now…"

"And now I don't know how to feel."

"Well take some time by yourself to think about things. Julius is a nice guy. I liked him. Whatever it is, I think you guys will be able to get through it together."

"You're such an optimist."

"I know. And it's annoying, but I like to believe in the best of everyone."

"Is that why you stayed married to Mom so long?"

"No. I was afraid if I left her, she would kill me. Literally."

"Knowing Mom, that was a pretty valid fear."

We both laughed. He patted my hand then squeezed it. "Lori just pulled up with the champagne. Want to join us?"

I shook my head. "I think I'll make myself scarce. This is a special time. You guys go ahead and celebrate."

I stood and kissed my dad on the forehead. "Congrats. Lori's a lucky woman."

I was heading down the walkway as Lori climbed out of her car.

"Hey! Where are you going? I have champagne," she said, waving a bottle at me.

I couldn't help but smile. Lori was going to make a nice addition to our family.

I hugged her, surprising her, and she gave a surprised laugh. "Welcome to the family, Lori. Thanks for putting up with my dad."

"Ha! I should thank him for putting up with me."

And with that, she made her way into the house.

I could see them embrace in front of the window. I couldn't believe it. Dad found his own version of happily ever after.

I didn't know where else to go, so I drove over to Dana's place. She wasn't home, and I was tempted to pop up where she worked, but I didn't want to risk running into Douglas.

I didn't want to go back home, and I didn't want to bother Piper. Everyone was busy. I felt pretty alone. I figured moments like these were when people would call their mothers, but I totally didn't want to do that. I wanted to feel better, not worse.

So I pulled up to a quaint bookshop and sat nosing through a magazine that I had no interest in buying. I didn't pay attention to anything I was reading. I was just turning the pages. I must have fallen asleep because what seemed like a few seconds later, someone was shaking my shoulder.

"Sorry to wake you, but you were snoring really loud," a teenager said with a bit of amusement in his eyes.

I looked around and saw people looking at me but pretending not to. I was sure I was blushing. "Sorry," I murmured and walked away, not making eye contact with anyone.

Now that I had officially embarrassed myself, I was

very much awake and feeling really put out. I didn't want to go home. I didn't want to bother Piper or Dana. And so like a sad character in a made for TV drama, I sat in my car and cried.

An hour later, I was done feeling sorry for myself so I drove past my dad's house to see if Lori was still there. There was no sign of her, so I went inside calling Dad's name as I did.

I noticed the note on the table and picked it up.

Went to Vegas to celebrate our engagement. See you in a few days! Dad.

"Oh man, I want to go to Vegas," I said to no one in particular. I wasn't done feeling sorry for myself.

I passed the next few days wearing a onesie that I normally only wore during Christmas season even though it wasn't anytime near Christmas and it was hot outside. I did nothing but sit in front of the television and watch reality TV shows. I ate chips and drank soda. I ignored the calls and texts I was getting from Julius. I couldn't talk to him right now. I didn't know how I felt about us.

It was nightfall when I heard someone knocking on the door. I had fallen asleep again; it seemed to be a habit of mine. Maybe I was depressed.

I got up and stumbled toward the door. "Who is it?" I said groggily. I had heard from Dad and knew not to expect him for another few days or so. I looked through the peephole and saw no one standing there. It was too dark.

I fumbled with the light switch and finally was able to turn on the light. A knock sounded again, and a demanding voice said, "Open the door. I'm causing a scene."

I opened the door only because I was in shock. What was she doing here?

Claire barged her way in and just started talking. "I can't find her. She's not answering my calls. She's not at the house. She's not at her apartment. She's not at his house. I don't know where she is. I need you to find her."

My brain had to wrap itself around the fact that Claire was in my house and barking orders at me.

"How did you know where I lived?"

"Google. Can you find her?" she said, sitting down and gripping her purse tightly. I could tell that she had been crying. Her eyes were puffy and red.

"Ana's missing?"

"Yes, child. Isn't that what I just said?"

I sat heavily and said exactly what I was thinking, "She's probably not missing. She's just avoiding you. Maybe she's tired of dealing with your craziness. I know I would be."

"My craziness?"

"Craziness. Insanity. Whatever you want to call it." I didn't censor myself. I was so over Claire and her nonsense. "Anyway, get out of my house. You're not welcome here."

"But I need your help."

"Don't care."

"But Ana needs you."

"I'm sure Ana is fine. The only thing she needs is for you to leave her alone. Leave her alone. Leave me alone. Get out."

"You don't have to be so rude."

"Claire, your entire existence is rude to the universe. Get out."

She looked ready to fight, but then her shoulders slumped and she started to cry. I didn't move to comfort her, but I did hand her a few tissues. As far as I was concerned, she was responsible for my unhappiness.

"I'm not a terrible person. I swear," she choked out, and I made a non-committal sound.

"I just want what's best for her."

"Yeah, really? Trying to sabotage your daughter's happiness doesn't sound like wanting the best for her."

"The whole engagement was a sham anyway."

I rolled my eyes. "Fine, keep making excuses for your behavior, and I'll keep eating chips. Get out."

"Do you know where she could be?"

"She's your daughter."

"She doesn't want to talk to me."

"The only person who might know where she is, is Julius. So go cry on his couch."

"He won't speak to me."

"Well, can you blame him?"

"I really messed things up."

"Yeah, trying to ruin your daughter's life doesn't exactly make you mother of the year." I felt like I was channeling Dana. That was totally something she would say.

"Why are you being so mean?"

"Mean?! You're the definition of mean."

"Do you think that's why Ana won't speak to me?"

"Yes! That's exactly why!" Was Claire really that dense when it came to human emotions? Apparently so.

Do you ever think she'll talk to me again?" she sobbed harder.

I thought about it. "Sure, on Christmas and maybe your birthday."

"She's all I have, Becca. She's everything to me."

"Then tell Ana that."

"She won't listen to me."

"You can't blame her for that. If I were in her shoes, I wouldn't want to hear anything you have to say."

"Thanks."

"I'm just being honest. You were pretty nasty the other day."

"I will admit, I was a bit unkind."

"A bit? You were terrible."

"I was," she said, sobbing again. "I've lost her. I'm a terrible mom, a terrible person."

I kept quiet. She already felt bad enough, there was no point in making her feel worse.

"What should I do?"

"Apologize."

"Okay."

"And then give her space."

"What if she doesn't accept my apology? What if she truly doesn't want anything to do with me anymore?"

"Ana loves you. Loves you so much that she'll do anything to please you, even making up a fake fiancé to do it. I don't think she'll ever cut you out of her life, but I think you do need to give her some space to think. She'll forgive you, just in her own time."

"Do you really think so?"

"Yep." I got up then and said, "Now, can you leave?"

She stood and stuck the tissue in her pocket. "Thank you for being so kind. I've been terrible toward you, and I'm sorry." The way her voice quivered made me think that apologizing wasn't exactly her forte.

"Don't worry about the money," she continued, "You earned that plus more just putting up with me."

Oh yeah, I had totally forgot that she wanted the money back. As if that was ever going to happen. Yeah right.

"I know I said a lot of harsh things, but I was wrong for saying those things. I know you're a good person. Better than most people I know. You're definitely a better person than I. I'm sorry for making your relationship with Julius seem…"

"Dirty?"

"Yes, I'm sorry for making you look like a—"

"Whore?"

She swallowed hard. "I… yes. I'm sorry."

I sighed. I was still angry with her, but that anger was misplaced. The person I was really mad at was myself, but I wasn't letting Claire know that.

"Thanks…"

And with that, she let herself out.

Sighing, I locked the door and sat back in my dad's recliner. Her words had at least taken away a little of the shame and pain I felt, but not all of it. It still hurt that I had done exactly what she had expected, gotten involved with Julius.

I didn't like to feel manipulated. And I hated that she knew me better than I knew myself. Even if it all was a ruse, I was so easily manipulated or rather not manipulated, I was exactly the person she thought me to be. And that was why I was so angry.

I snuggled under a blanket and tried to watch some more bad TV, but my stomach started to growl. I needed more junk. I stood and went rummaging through the kitchen cabinets and found another bag of chips and my dad's hidden stash of cookies. I figured they had probably gone stale, but whatever; cookies were for eating, expired or not.

"These cookies are so good," I murmured to myself while snuggling under the blanket. I pushed everything out of my head: Julius, finding my own place, everything, and just ate cookies and binged watched TV.

I was nodding off when I heard another knock on the door.

I groaned and made myself get up as the knocking became more insistent.

"Stop banging on my door, Claire!" I yelled, "Gosh!" I found my way to the door and looked through the peephole. I wanted to make sure a murderer wasn't trying to break down my door first.

Nope. I immediately squatted, scared that the unexpected visitor would see me through the peephole. It definitely wasn't a murderer.

It was Julius.

He knocked again, and I yelled, "Go away."

"Come on, Becca. Let me in."

"No."

"Come on."

"Go away."

"I just want to talk to you."

"No!"

"Please open the door."

I stayed quiet hoping he would go away. A minute passed and then another. And I stood up a little to look out the window. He was peering through that exact window, and I screamed, startled.

"Sorry," he said, and I heard him laugh.

I couldn't help but smile too.

"Come on, Becca, let me in before someone calls the cops."

I stood and had my hand on the doorknob as I turned the lock.

I slowly opened the door just a crack.

"Can I come in?"

I stared at him, not realizing until that moment how much I missed him.

And it was for that reason that I didn't want to let him in. I knew if I opened the door and he crossed the threshold, there wasn't any turning back. I would be under his spell, but maybe that wasn't necessarily a bad thing.

"If you let me in, I'll be on my best behavior."

"I don't believe you."

He pretended to actually consider his next response before saying, "I promise."

I opened the door, hoping I wasn't making a huge mistake.

He came in quietly and took off the baseball cap he

was wearing. It seemed like he had gotten dress in a hurry. He was wearing sweatpants and a hoodie.

"I've been texting you, calling you; what's going on?"

I sat down wearily. "I just don't know how I feel about us anymore."

He sat heavily across from me and removed his hoodie. His hair was sticking up all over his head, and it looked like he hadn't shaved in a while.

"Are you sick or something?" I asked, concerned.

"Do I look that bad?" he asked, looking up and rubbing his beard. "I'm not sick. I was just worried about you when you wouldn't answer my calls."

"Gosh, now you sound like Claire."

"You talked to Claire?"

"She stopped by upset that Ana isn't talking to her. yelling that she was missing."

"Ana isn't missing, I just saw her."

Silence settled between us.

"Is she okay?"

"She's fine. She just needs some space. Standing up to her mom really drained her. She's never done it before."

"She did a great job."

"She did. I was proud of her."

"Me too."

"So why haven't you returned my calls?"

"I just felt bad—really bad—about what happened between us."

"Why would you feel bad about that?"

"She set us up, Julius, and we fell for it; who wouldn't feel bad about that? She assumed the worst of us, and we proved her to be right."

He shook his head. "So she orchestrated us meeting, and she counted on us being attracted to each other. Claire is calculating and mean, but she's also perceptive. She noticed what was between us and capitalized on it."

"Exactly."

"But we fell for each other on our own terms. She didn't manipulate that."

He had a point, but I wasn't interested in logic. I was upset still. I didn't plan to let myself off the hook that easily. For some reason, it seemed that I wanted to be angry.

"Why are you still angry with me?"

"I don't know. I'm just confused. I don't know how to feel. I'm just a complicated mess."

"Love isn't complicated," he said, standing then coming to sit next to me. "You either want to be with me or you don't. Claire has nothing to do with how I feel about you, Becca. I love you."

Everything he said made sense. All of it. I knew that I loved Julius, but I was also afraid. He was right. Claire had nothing to do with this.

And as I found myself climbing into his lap, Claire and her nonsense were the furthest things on my mind.

We made love on the couch and after we were both spent, he told me that he loved me again.

I reacted badly, telling him that he didn't love me and that I couldn't love him. He walked out the door, and I sat there and cried. What had gotten into me? What was wrong with me? Why hadn't I stopped him from leaving? Why had I denied the love we felt for each other?

I didn't know what was wrong with me. I didn't have any answers, and I didn't know what to do next.

9

I sat next to Dana feeling totally in awe of her. The website she had created for me looked amazing.

"Wow, Dana. Seriously, just wow. This is impressive. Absolutely amazing."

"Well, don't just thank me, Mac and Douglas helped too."

I arched a brow at the mention of Douglas. "How's he doing, by the way? Still madly in love with his ex?"

Dana shot me an apologetic look. "Very much so. Except she's not his ex anymore. I think they're getting married soon. I think seeing you with him was a reality check for her."

"Of course," I said bitterly.

Dana looked guilty. "Sorry about that, again. Next

time I hook you up with someone, I'll make sure that they're very single."

"There won't be a next time," I said shortly. Dana didn't know all the details about what had happened between Julius and me, and I really didn't plan to tell her, but I didn't want her to get any bright ideas about setting me up with someone else.

"Did you call him back?"

I pretended to not know what she was talking about. "Call who back?"

"That guy who has been calling you nonstop since you got here. I'm guessing that's Julius. Why don't you call him? What did the poor guy do that was so terrible?"

"No," I said grumpily. "I'm not calling him back."

"Someone's in love," Dana said in a sing-song voice.

I rolled my eyes. "I thought you were supposed to be the mature one."

"Maturity is overrated," she said, changing the subject as she asked me about fonts and color choices for my website.

I couldn't get over her, "Someone's in love," comment. I wasn't in love. I was, but it wasn't as if it was noticeable. Or was it? What did someone in love look like?

When Dad had fallen in love with Lori, he walked

around with more confidence. He smiled more, and I would catch him sometimes just sitting around whistling. He had become a whole new person. It was almost as if the weight of love had relieved some of his stress and anxiety of life. That was what love did—it made life better.

And truth be told, I felt different when I fell for Julius. I felt more optimistic and the world seemed like less of a scary place. But if that was true, why was I still ignoring his calls and pretending he didn't exist? Even I couldn't figure me out.

"Dana," I said with hesitation in my voice, "how did you know that you were in love with Carter?"

She smiled. "Because even after years of not seeing him, when he showed up again, the world just seemed brighter. It was as if his presence made up for all the crap that was going on around me. Excuse me for not being very poetic, but his mere existence made my heart sing."

I nodded. "Yeah, that sounds like love."

Dana studied me, but didn't say anything for a long while. "If you think you're in love, just go for it."

"But what if I'm wrong? What if it doesn't work out?"

She shrugged "Then, oh well, at least you tried. Now how about this font? It's one of my favorites. I think it says artistic yet sexy. What do you think?"

I murmured in agreement, but my mind was elsewhere. Did Julius make my heart sing?

After I left Dana's office, I stopped by Piper's place. She and her husband, Ty, asked me to stop by to go over my business plan. Ty ran a successful dating agency and that was actually how he had met Piper. They were both successful entrepreneurs, so I was thrilled that they were taking time out of their busy schedules to give me advice.

But when I got to Piper's place, the first thing she said to me was, "Oh my gosh! I heard you've fallen in love."

I groaned. Couldn't a girl have a little privacy? Apparently not with best friends like Piper and Dana.

I tried to deflect. "Didn't you want to see me about my business plan?"

"The business plan looks great," Piper said. "Tell me about this Julius character. He sounds like a Roman deity. Is he built like one too?"

I could either dodge the question and then spend the next half an hour dodging similar questions, or I could just give her the rundown.

"I love him. He loves me. Yes, he reminds me of a minor deity. Kind of like a young Thor. No, we're not together right now. No, I don't know why. The end. Now can we talk about my business plan?"

She looked disappointed, but luckily Ty walked in at that very moment. "Becca, great, you're here already. I thought I heard your voice. Love the business plan, but I have a few questions—"

He stopped abruptly when he realized that Piper was giving him a dirty look.

"What did I say?" he asked, looking from me to Piper, puzzled.

"Nothing, Ty, Piper is just being nosey and inquiring about my love life."

Ty raised his hands as if to ward off evil demons. "Then I'll leave you two to it."

"No!" I said more forcefully than I should have. "I don't want to talk about my love life. I just want to focus on my career. That's all I can handle right now." I was tearing up, and I didn't know why.

Piper handed me a tissue. "Oh, Becca, I'm sorry. I didn't mean to make you cry. Are you sure you don't want to talk about it?"

I shook my head. "No. I just want to talk about my business plan. I don't want to talk about love. Or men. Or anything. Just business. Okay?"

Piper looked ready to argue, but Ty shot her a look.

"Sure, Becca," Ty said. "That's fine. Just business. Okay, Piper? Just business."

Piper looked at me and then at Ty and sighed, "Fine."

God, I needed a break from so many prying questions. I just really needed a break from love.

* * *

"SO DO YOU HAVE A NEW BOYFRIEND?" Meredith asked as I helped her look over her sheet music for her next play. I shook my head. It was the next day, but it seemed I just couldn't get away from conversations directly, or indirectly, related to my love life.

We were at a park near her home. We hadn't spent a lot of time together since the whole Julius and Ana debacle, so I was trying to make up for that by taking her to the park and practicing music with her.

"What makes you think I have a boyfriend?" I asked.

She shrugged. "I don't know. You just seem, you know, happier. Sort of like when Mom got together with Carter."

I thought about her comment and Dana's comment from the day before. I guessed that was what love did to you, even when you couldn't really act on it. Love made the world seem brighter. It made you happier. That was why love was so powerful. And I knew that was why I couldn't resist Julius. I loved him. It was as simple as that. I was in love with Julius. I couldn't tell him that or rather, I wouldn't tell him that. I hadn't actually spoken to him since the night we made love on the sofa. I was too scared to speak to him. I couldn't trust myself.

He called over and over. He texted me and even

emailed me, but I ignored all his attempts at communicating with me.

I was also ignoring Claire. I didn't care if Ana never spoke to her again; that was Ana's decision, not mine.

I realized that Meredith was waiting for me to say something. "You know if I had a boyfriend, you would be the first person I would tell."

"Really?" Her tone was dubious.

"Yes, really."

"You promise?"

"Pinky swear."

She smiled. "You would be the first person I would tell. I wouldn't tell Mom. She would freak out. I would probably tell Carter. He's the more rational one of the two."

I held back my laughter, but she was right. I knew Dana would flip out if she knew Meredith was even talking about boys. She barely tolerated Meredith's best friend, Danny. Speaking of which, I wondered if Danny might know what was going on with his great aunt and her daughter. I was trying to think of a subtle way to ask Meredith when someone tapped on my shoulder.

I turned around, half expecting Julius to be standing there, but no, even worse. It was Ana.

"Hi," I said, giving her a tight smile. I hadn't seen her since the picture incident at her mother's house. I still wanted to hide my face in shame at the thought of them.

She smiled back and said, "I was just taking a walk and saw you two hanging out and thought to say hello. Is this your niece?"

"No, this is Meredith. My stepdaughter."

"Stepdaughter, best friend, partner in crime, I fulfill all those roles plus more," Meredith said ,extending her hand for Ana to shake.

"What a precocious young lady you are," Ana said with a smile. "Well, it's nice to meet you, Meredith."

"You too." Meredith then looked from me to Ana. "How do you guys know each other?"

"I was the photographer for her engagement party," I said, shooting Meredith a meaningful look. Meredith sort of knew the whole story, or at least g-rated bits and pieces. Meredith's mouth formed a perfect O, but she smiled politely and said, "Oh, cool."

I breathed a sigh of relief. Sometimes Meredith volunteered a little too much information. I was glad this wasn't one of those times.

"Can I talk to you for a second? In private?" Ana asked, and I desperately wanted to shout, "No!"

Where had all my bravery gone? Now I was behaving like a coward. Courage wasn't my strong point.

We walked to a spot under a tree, where I could still see Meredith, but we were out of earshot, so she couldn't eavesdrop. Ana started, "Julius told me that he—"

Oh god. Oh god. Oh god. I didn't want to talk about Julius. I felt like my head was about to explode.

"…told you about Sam."

I frowned. Sam? This conversation was about Sam?

I nodded. "I'm sorry. I had no idea."

She looked down at her hands. "Sam was one of my best friends. And when he died, it was almost as if part of me died with him. I know how trite that must sound, but it's true."

I didn't interrupt. I wanted to hear what she had to say.

"Julius was there for me through it all. And I knew he was hurting too, but he was strong for both of us." She looked up from her hands, but still didn't meet my eyes.

"What I'm trying to say is that Julius has always been there when I needed him the most. But I can't say I did the same in return."

She hung her head in shame, and I couldn't help but feel for her.

I tried to make her feel better saying, "I know he values you as a friend."

She looked up and shook her head. "I've been a terrible friend. Always taking and never giving. Always making things about me." She gave a bitter laugh. "I've turned into my mom."

"You're definitely not your mother," I said fiercely.

Ana laughed and then shrugged. "In some ways, I am. But now I'm seeing that's not necessarily a bad thing."

She continued, "Anyway, Mom and I will figure things out; we always do. I'm just more worried about you and Julius."

"We're not... I don't..."

"He's in love with you."

Words of denial got stuck in my throat. "Did he tell you that?"

She nodded. "And you're in love with him. So why are you pushing him away?"

I didn't have an answer. Why was I pushing him away? There was nothing stopping us from being together. Nothing at all. I was the only thing standing between us. Well, not me, just my stupidity. I could see that now.

"When Sam died, Julius was there for me. When I felt my life had no meaning, Julius stepped in and showed me how much more I had to live for. When I couldn't stand up to my mother and created this whole crazy, elaborate, fake engagement, Julius still stood by me instead of telling me that I was crazy... which I was. That's the kind of man Julius is, Becca. He'll do anything for the people he loves. Now I don't know what's stopping you from building a life with him, but don't make the same mistake I did."

I looked at her sharply. What was she talking about? The same mistake… what did that mean?

"Sam died without ever knowing how I felt about him. I loved him so much. And I was his roommate! I had plenty of chances to tell him!" she said with a regretful laugh. "I could have told him any day. At any time. I didn't have the courage, and now he's gone. And I don't know if I'll love anyone again like I loved him. And what I'm trying to say is… I don't know. Just don't take Julius' love for granted. Tomorrow isn't promised to anyone. If you love him, be with him. Don't let whatever hang-ups you have from your past stop you from being with the person you love."

She wiped away a tear. "Okay, speech over," she said with a shaky laugh.

"I don't know what to say."

"And I have nothing else to say, soooo…"

We both laughed this time.

I took her hand in mine and squeezed it before letting go. "Thanks for talking sense into me."

She smiled. "Anytime." She then looked over at Meredith who was singing softly to herself. "And if your stepdaughter ever needs any help with her vocals, give me a call. I mean, I am the lead singer of a band."

"You're singing again?" I asked in surprise.

Now it was Ana's turn to look surprised. "So I guess Julius mentioned the band?"

"Yeah, but I thought you didn't sing anymore."

"I'm done being a shadow of my former self. That's not the life Sam would have wanted for me. I think we can both agree on that."

I nodded, hearing the wisdom in her words.

"Now, call Julius," she commanded, sounding very much like her mother. "He's driving me crazy. He keeps sending me these pitiful pics of himself at home, looking depressed."

She showed me one, and we both winced.

"He looks terrible," we said at the same time.

"Go cheer him up. I think he would like that kind of surprise."

She gave me one last hug then she walked away from us.

"What did she want?" Meredith asked.

"To talk some sense into me."

Meredith eyed me. "Well, did it work?"

I smiled. "I think it did."

After I dropped Meredith off, I went home, showered, and put on some decent clothes. I then headed to Julius' home. I took a deep breath and knocked on the door. What if he didn't want to see me? What if he didn't answer the door? What if—

"What are you doing here?" Julius asked as he opened the door. His hair was sticking up everywhere and his voice sounded husky as if he had just woken up. It was three o'clock in the afternoon. What was he doing sleeping? He had a tortilla chip stuck to his stomach. I flicked it off.

"Hey," he said, looking upset, "I was eating that."

I shook my head. Had I really had this effect on the poor guy?

"Aren't you going to invite me in?"

He narrowed his eyes at me. "That depends." He yawned before continuing, "Why do you want me to invite you in? So that you can stomp all over my heart again. No thanks."

He tried to close the door, and I caught it. "I'm sorry I've been so stupid."

His eyebrows shot up. "I'm listening."

I shrugged. "That's all I got. I'm sorry I've been so stupid. And I want to be a part of your life. I want to grow old with you. Marry you. Have your babies."

He stopped me. "Hold on a second there. Let's not get ahead of ourselves. How about we start with going out to dinner as an official couple or something?"

"That sounds like a pretty good plan."

He scratched his chest. "Life with you will be very interesting, Becca."

"Interesting is better than boring, right?"

"I don't know," he said, leaning against his doorframe and scratching his head. I thought he was finally waking up. "Someone once told me that I was the most boring person she ever knew."

"I like boring," I said, moving closer to him and wrapping my arms around his neck. He didn't try to stop me, so I moved closer until our lips were just inches apart. "Boring is sexy."

"Oh is it now?" he said, smiling down at me.

I nodded.

"Is it okay if this boring guy tells you that he loves you?"

I pretended to consider it. "I guess... just this one time..."

"I love you, Becca."

"I love you too, Julius."

"Finally, you admit it. It's about damn time..."

He lowered his head and kissed me. And he was right, it was about damn time.

EPILOGUE

"I can't believe I'm doing this again," I said to Meredith.

"I know! Isn't this exciting?" She made the prettiest bridesmaid. Aquamarine was definitely her color.

I looked in the mirror. I didn't make too bad of a bride. I opted out of the traditional white dress and went for an off-white gown that sort of hid the baby weight that I hadn't exactly shed in the past six months since the baby was born.

Julius and I hadn't exactly done things in order, but that hadn't meant I was going to be deprived of the wedding of my dreams: an intimate, small wedding on the beach.

It was a perfect day. The weather had cooperated. The sun was shining but not oppressive. And there was a breeze in the air. Everything I wanted with the man I couldn't have asked more from. Dad was right. Julius was definitely a winner.

And as if reading my mind, Dad peeked his head in and the music began to play. "That's our cue, lovely lady," he said, extending his elbow to me.

I took it and gave him a smile. Dad looked so handsome in his pale linen suit. I loved him so much. He was great and helpful with all the wedding plans. He even spoke to Mom which was a huge deal. She wasn't attending. She said she had a previous engagement. I didn't know what was more important than seeing her oldest child get married, but I knew better than to get upset. Mom would always be Mom.

As Dad and I positioned ourselves to walk down the aisle, I realized that my heart was racing, but not from excitement. I was kind of scared. Of what? I didn't know. After all, Julius and I had already been together for three years before we had our son Julius Jr., J.J. for short. I knew Julius was a great father. He was also my best friend. He meant everything to me. So what was I so afraid of?

Meredith and my other bridesmaids, Piper, Dana, and Ana, started down the white runner that led to the perfect spot on the beach where Julius and I were to be married.

And then it was our turn.

"You ready?" Dad asked me.

I looked down the aisle and saw Julius standing there. Lori, my stepmom, held JJ who was blowing raspberries nonstop. Julius reached out and kissed his son's forehead before turning back to look in my direction.

The moment he spotted me, he smiled.

"I'm ready," I said with certainty. I wasn't afraid anymore. And as Dad walked me down the aisle, I didn't notice the onlookers around me. I didn't notice our guests. All I saw was Julius. The father of my child and my best friend. I knew everyone had said it, but at that moment, I felt like the luckiest woman in the whole world.

And I guessed that was because I was.

Dad handed me off to Julius, and he raised my veil.

"Are you crying?" he asked, wiping away a tear.

"No," I said and then confessed a second later, "Okay, yes."

"Tears of joy, I hope," Julius said with a smile.

I couldn't help myself as I leaned forward and kissed him.

He laughed when I pulled away. "Hon, the kiss is supposed to be at the end of the wedding."

"I won't tell if you don't."

"We all saw it," Dana said. Of course she would interrupt a sweet moment.

Julius took my hand in his. "Are you ready to become Mrs. Julius Romo?"

"She better be," my dad commented. "This wedding isn't paying for itself." And then he laughed. Lori pinched him, and he winced.

Lori was also officiating the ceremony. Who would have known that Lori was also an ordained minister?

She beamed up at us. "Are you love birds ready to be united in holy matrimony?"

"Sounds like a plan," I quipped.

Julius smiled down at me and took my other hand in his as we turned to face each other.

"I love you," I said for his ears alone.

"I love you too," he said, pulling me closer.

I felt a small chubby hand clawing at my face. I guess J.J. also wanted his mom's attention. I kissed his hand, and he giggled.

I couldn't imagine a happier moment. I was the luckiest woman in the world today. I was marrying my soulmate surrounded by family, friends, and most importantly, love.

DARK DESIRES
~ A billionaire dark romance series ~
Dark Desire
Dark Rules
Dark Secret
Dark Time
Dark Truth

BARRE TO BAR
~ A billionaire second chance series ~
Dancing With Lies
Dancing With Temptation
Dancing With Doubt
Dancing With Guilt
Dancing With Redemption

TWISTED INTENTION
~ A billionaire revenge romance series ~
Twisted Beauty
Twisted Love
Twisted Fate

Mafia's Obsession
~ A hot mafia romance series ~
Mafia's Dirty Secret
Mafia's Fake Bride
Mafia's Final Play

Screaming Demons
~ An MC romance series full of suspense ~
Rough Start
Rough Ride
Rough Choice
Rough Patch
Rough Return
Rough Road
Rough Trip
Rough Night
Rough Love

Standalone Contemporary Romance
Billionaire in Vegas
Billionaire Hunt

Billionaire's Game
Billionaire Retreat
Billionaire On Air
A Chance To Love
Somebody To Love
Not Mine To Love

Check out Summer's entire collection at
www.summercooper.com/books

ABOUT SUMMER COOPER

Thank you so much for reading. Without you, it wouldn't be possible for me to be a full-time author. I hope you enjoy reading my books as much as I do writing them.

Besides (obviously!) reading and writing, I also love cuddling my dogs, shouting at Alexa, being upside down (aka Yoga) and driving my family cray-cray!

Get in touch at
hello@summercooper.com
www.summercooper.com

facebook.com/summercooperauthor
instagram.com/summercooperauthor
goodreads.com/summercooper
bookbub.com/profile/summer-cooper